Deception in the Details

A Novel — Book Two

AVAGAYE CLARKE-HERON

INSPIRE PUBLICATIONS

minna PRESS

ISBN: 978-1-7324034-8-2

Ordering Information
Quantity (Bulk) Sales: Special discounts are available on quantity (bulk) purchases by corporations, associations, and others. For details, contact: InSpirePublications1@gmail.com

Executive Editor: Lena J. Rose
Designer: Mark Steven Weinberger

Published in the U.S.A.

Dedication

I dedicate this book to my husband Ricardo Heron, my main support system, whose impressive dedication to self-advancement and believing in one's dreams inspired me to believe that I was capable of authoring a book. To my dear son Aiden Heron who I have been immensely blessed with, and to my dear mother, without whose encouragement, drive and unwavering love, I would not have had the confidence and drive to pursue my dreams.

Acknowledgement

I would like to express my appreciation to the many people who made the completion of this novel possible; to all those who provided support, offered comments, and assisted in the editing, proofreading and design.

I would like to thank my publisher, Lena J. Rose, for her assistance in publishing this book. Above all, I want to thank my husband, Ricardo Heron as well as my son, Aiden Heron and the rest of my family, who supported and encouraged me along the way.

I would like to especially thank my good friends Shanakaye Royal-Johnson, Gaynor Hunter-Wong, Sydia Shaw and Tamara Ebanks for their never-ending support and confidence in me. They have all played a significant role in my perseverance towards the completion of this book series.

Last but not least; I would like to thank all those friends, colleagues, and well-wishers who have been with me over the course of the years and whose names I have failed to mention

Chapter I

On the drive to Liz's new home a strange silence settled in the car. Liz had asked Kayla why she stayed back to speak to James and Kayla told her she would tell her as soon as they got home.

"Liz I'm so excited that we are now free to be together."

"Hmm…" Liz said on a heavy exhale, looking straight ahead. The silence thickened and stretched.

Kayla knew what was eating Liz up inside but didn't know how to start.

"Take the right at the next intersection," Liz said in a gloomy tone. "It's the third house on the left. This is one of the properties my dad left behind," she added, as if she felt the awkwardness too. "You can pull up there in the driveway."

Kayla backed up the car in the driveway, Liz quickly got out and started unloading her things into the garage, Kayla could see from the look on her face that she was upset. She was desperate to clear the air. "Liz," she said grabbing onto Liz's hand as she tried to take the last box from the trunk of the car. "At least let me help you with this one because it's a bit heavy." Liz looked at her, almost stating in her eyes that she didn't need her help, but Kayla held onto the box anyway helping her to lay it down in the garage. "I said I would tell you why I wanted to talk to James alone when we got home, and now we are home, you don't need to be mad at me because I *will* tell you." Liz threw her a skeptic look. "Trust me, I don't want to start the rest of our lives together with secrets because I know how dangerous that can be, please just let us go inside and I'll explain everything."

Liz pulled the garage door, hard, and strode to the front of the house to open the door. As she walked, her shoulders were visibly tense, which made her back arch slightly. Kayla followed behind her inside. "This is nice," Kayla said looking around at the picturesque, contemporary layout of Liz's sitting room. "Seems you have already made it ready to move in," she added, as she continued to observe the décor. The ash-grey laminate flooring anchored the white leather sofas flanked by a marble fireplace. A uniquely abstract-shaped coffee table stood in the middle of the room, and on top of the glass side tables were gorgeous lotus shaped lamps. Everything tied in beautifully with the luxurious, jasmine white drapes and almond white walls.

"Yeah," Liz replied with a dispassionate glance at the room. "I spent a few evenings here during the divorce process, fixing it up, making it ready for the kids. It wasn't much work to do, just a bit of dusting and re-shifting the furniture to my liking. It was one of those houses my dad would lease out, but I'm going to be using it for now because it's more of a family house than the others." After another drawn out pause, Liz cleared her throat. "So, should I get you something to drink?"

Kayla nodded to say yes, but Liz had already walked off to the kitchen. Kayla made her to way to the sitting area and sat on the edge of the couch. Liz came walking in with a bottle of red wine in one hand and two wine glasses in the other.

"Wine?" Kayla said looking at her, "well it definitely suits the occasion," she mumbled under her breath."

"What?" Liz was jumpy, a pained expression on her face.

"It's nothing," Kayla responded promptly; "I'd love some wine." Liz poured the wine and she sat on the couch next to Kayla.

Liz sloshed the wine a bit in the glass, took a sniff and sipped. "Well," she said, "since you are waiting for me to ask again… why you wanted to talk to James alone… you wanna tell me what is going on?"

Kayla took a sip from her own glass and looked at Liz. "For you to understand why I had to speak to James alone, you first need to know how it started."

"When you and I first met at *WhisPer*, you had asked me what was my story, I didn't know you then like I do now, so I didn't open up to you about my past. You told me then that the people you knew came to *WhisPer* to escape their realities and you were right. I was there because I was trying to somehow mend my broken heart. "You see," she shifted uncomfortably on the couch, "back in Vancouver, I met a guy, his name was Jay."

"What the heck does this have to do with you wanting to talk to James alone?" Liz interrupted, her eyes glared at Kayla.

"Just let me finish. It will all make sense if you'd just let me explain. Liz made a gesture as to say fine and Kayla continued to speak. "I met a guy in the coffee shop I stopped by every morning before I went to work, the lady at the coffee shop would normally have my coffee waiting for me at the same time every morning as she knew exactly what I needed. Decaf, one pump of hazel nut creamer and two blocks of sugar. One morning, I went in and it was packed, I signaled to Martha, the owner of the coffee shop, and she took up my coffee and placed it on the counter for me. Then out of nowhere this guy I had never seen in the shop before just walked up and held on to it. I assumed he was mistaking it for his, so I walked up to him and told him it was my coffee, he took a sip from it and said "no that's my coffee, 'decaf, one pump of hazel nut creamer and two blocks of sugar, just the way I like it.' I was a little taken aback that he had the same preference but I pointed to the cup where my name was clearly written on the side, close to the lid as Martha always did."

"He apologized, but was a little cynical, and I was pissed that he drank my coffee so I just turned around and walked out of the shop. I forgot all about it until a week later he showed up at my office offering to buy me another coffee and apologizing for his first impression at the coffee shop. Pretty soon I realized that the first impression I had of him was not right. He was sweet, considerate and he was not just another guy trying to get into my pants; at least that was what I thought then. Over time, as we kept seeing each other, we would talk about everything and he would listen and remember details. We dated on and off for the first two years and then things got more serious. We started sleeping with each other. I had things at his place and he left things at my condo. He told me he was an IT Consultant and that's why he travelled as often as he did, working with a number of companies in different countries. Frankly, it didn't bother me, and I didn't think much of it because it made our relationship exciting. When he was away, I would long for him, and when he came back the sex would be so amazing because we had time apart to miss each other."

I dated Jay for six years, and the longest he would stay out of Vancouver during that time was six months at a time. But then, he told me he had to go away for a family emergency for two years or more to take care of his family business and to support his brother who was going through a divorce. He suggested that we could see other people during that time apart, and that he would understand if I couldn't wait for him. Though I didn't know what our relationship would be like after that we still maintained our relationship over the phone. He would send me gifts on my birthday, and other special occasions and he convinced me to wait for him.

Six years of dating and two years of long-distance relationship, I was all in for this man for eight years, and when he came back to Vancouver I was convinced that he came back to marry me. I mean, if he didn't love me he could have blown me off when he went away, why come back? Why have me wait for him? After he had been back for some months, one weekend he told me he was taking me somewhere special. I felt within my heart that he was going to propose. He took me to a cabin by a beautiful lake, romanced me for the entire weekend, and on the morning, at the end of the weekend I got up with my hopes up ready for him to propose, only to find a note telling me that he went back to his wife and kids." Kayla broke down at this point and covered her face with her hands. Liz kept on staring at her in stony silence.

"I was devastated to say the least," she sniffled, letting her hands fall. "No one deserves to be used like that you know? I was hurt, I was angry, I was bitter, I was mad, even more so at myself for being so naïve and blinded by love. So, I took this promotion in California to start over; to try to get over the hurt, which for some time seemed impossible, because everywhere I went there was something that reminded me of him and how lonely and broken I was. "And then, I met you Liz, and I slowly started to be happy again, I started to heal, and I forgot about what Jay did to me until that night that you asked me to tail James for you."

Chapter 2

"I don't understand. What happened when you tailed James?" Liz asked looking all confused.

"Liz there is no easy way to say this... but Jay... the guy who deceived me and took me for a ride, is your James... and I swear to you on my mother's grave, I did not know until that night I tailed James and to my surprise James was... Jay... James... oh, you know what I mean."

Liz sat her glass down on the table and looked at Kayla almost speechless.

"Say something!" Kayla said, holding onto Liz's hand.

"I hated her..." Liz responded with a look on her face as if she was staring into the past.

"Hated who?" Kayla asked confused.

"You, her, that woman who stole my husband's love away from me, I hated her, I hated you. Now you are telling me that you are that woman." Liz was near hysterical and turning beet red.

Kayla tried to calm her... "Liz, I was deceived by James too, please understand, when I met him I had no idea he was married, I told you the story of how we met for you to understand that I didn't even pursue this man. He found me, he made me love him, he took eight years of my life and threw it all into a blender along with my heart and liquefied it to nothing." She knelt in front of Liz. Please believe me when I tell you that if I had known that he was married I wouldn't have spent eight years loving this man... this should change nothing between us."

Liz got up from her seat, pacing around just trying to take it all in, then she just started to laugh. "Isn't it ironic? The Gods are indeed having a field day with my love life. What are the odds that the woman I hated for so long, that I thought about killing many times, the woman I lost my husband's love to is the woman that I fell in love with without even knowing it. God this is messed up on so many levels."

"I know this is messed up," Kayla said walking towards her, "and trust me when I found out I had so many mixed feelings about what this would mean for us. But Liz, how can you say he loved me, he didn't, he used me! Just like he used you, and Celia, and God knows how many others. He made me believe he was mine when all along he was married to you. He is sleeping with your family lawyer for God sakes, he didn't love me, so please don't say that."

Liz sat back down on the sofa and took another sip of her wine. "You don't understand," she said, "he loved you, the only reason he broke it off with her... with you... was because I made him, I gave him an ultimatum, break it off or lose everything...

remember? He resented me after that and I believe that's why he went on this serial cheating to get back at me somehow for having him on a leash. I know my husband, and when he started the affair in Vancouver with you was the first time I knew I had lost him. You know the story Kayla, he changed... he didn't care for me anymore, he was risking his marriage, and his family to be with you. That's not just a silly affair, that's deeper than that. A silly affair is the one he was having with our lawyer, he didn't love her; it was just sex, to fill a need that I was not satisfying because I was still hurt that he didn't just have an affair with you, he fell in love."

Kayla sat beside Liz and took the glass from her, laying it back down on the coffee table. "None of that matters," she said to Liz. For all we know, you may have been reading too much into his 'supposed' love for me. I was on the other end, and I may have believed that then, but now I know it was just deception. Who forgets to tell someone, they claim to love, that they have a wife? When he dumped me in that note he left me at the cabin, he told me that when he met me he was going through a divorce, but if that was true why not say it then, why hide it? And judging from your story, when we met he was in Vancouver for the restructuring of your dad's companies not because he was going through a divorce like he said. Don't you get it? He never loved me. He was lying to me from the beginning, even before you gave him an ultimatum and that's not love in my book. So, again, I ask you, please stop saying that he loved me. The only reason I wanted to speak to him alone was to see the look on his face when he saw that we were together. I wanted to stick it to him, to point out the cosmic karma that was hitting him in the ass for what he did to me and that was it. If I had made you stay back while I said this to him you would have assumed the worst without knowing the entire story. I used to love Jay... James... whatever his name is, but now all I have in my heart for him is hate. I love you, and all I want is to be with you. Please don't let this change what we have found in each other, for each other. Please don't let the man that hurt us both be the one to come between us, or to change what we feel for each other."

Liz knew Kayla was right, and if she was completely honest with herself she would admit that it was satisfying to know how much more James would be hurting now that he knew she had not only left him with nothing but left him for the woman he broke their marriage for. The thought secretly made her smile inside, among other things that were brewing in her mind. She looked Kayla squarely in the face. "You are right. He used us both. It would be unfair to blame you for any of this because you were the victim; whether he had truly loved you is insignificant because it was based on deception. Let's just forget about James for now, we know we haven't heard the last of him, so let's just not work ourselves up about him until we have to deal with him."

Kayla hugged and kissed her in a gesture of relief. She was happy that Liz was willing to understand, and to forget about it and just move on with their lives without reliving James's deception drama.

Even though Kayla was relieved, she couldn't help but think that Liz handled the situation better than she had imagined.

She had seemed so level-headed about it even while voicing her concerns. She quickly shrugged the thought from her mind as she told herself she was overthinking it. She spent the rest of the evening helping Liz to unpack and just enjoying each other's company, basking in the feeling of finally being free to be together.

Chapter 3

James did not sleep well that night, he sat on the sofa in the living room just gazing at the television but not hearing a word, drinking glass after glass of bourbon. He couldn't make sense of it all, Kayla and Elizabeth. How was Kayla and Elizabeth together, how did they even meet? How was it that Kayla was the one who got evidence of him cheating with Celia? Was Liz and Kayla working together to make his life miserable, does Liz know that Kayla was the one he cheated with back in Vancouver? There were so many questions on his mind but no answers and it made him miserable. He gazed over at his phone, and noted the constant message notifications and missed calls but he didn't care. He laid down on the couch hugging the bourbon bottle. "Damn you Elizabeth!" He screamed, jumping up and tossing the bottle across the room. "Damn you!"

He made his way up the stairs, staggering, sweaty and confused. He needed to speak to Kayla, but how to do it was the question. Where would he start? He plopped himself down in bed, his head pounding, and stomach churning from the drinking. His eyes slowly dimmed, and he passed out.

A loud pounding on the door woke him up, and the sudden jolt of his head as he tried to rise, left a hammering ache on the left side of his head. He grabbed his phone to look at the time, it was 5:30 am. He held his hand to his head where the pain was as he walked over to the closet to get a shirt. He managed to throw on the shirt and made his way downstairs. The knocking at the door only got louder. "I'm coming!" he shouted, as he made his way towards the door. When he opened the door it was Celia. Her emotions were not easily hidden on her innocent-looking face. Pain was evident in her honey-brown eyes and in the downward curve of her full lips.

"What are you doing here?" he asked, grabbing her by the hand and pulling her in. He looked over her head to make sure no one saw her enter his house. Before she could respond, he said, "This is against the rules" as he closed the door. "You know my house is off limits."

"That was when you were legally married." Celia pulled her hand from his grasp. "Besides, I have been calling, and leaving messages for you to call me back, for over two days now, and you haven't picked up any of my calls or called me back."

"Really?" James looked at her annoyed. "You expect me to have a clear head to take calls, and have small talks with my mistress after everything that has happened over the last couple of months. Are you crazy?"

"I'm not the one that is crazy James, your wife is. I received an email from her, she's threating to have me subpoenaed by the Supreme Court. It's not bad enough that she is suing me for violation of trust and alienation, and a hoard of other things;

she's going after my credentials. She's trying to have me disbarred for desecration of the ethics of my profession."

James sat down, looking up at her in disbelief. "Can she do that?" What a pickle they have gotten themselves in; he was almost feeling sorry for her.

"Technically, yes, she can, because you both were my clients, and were legally married. I was trusted to advise you both, based on the ethical code(s) I operated under as a divorce attorney, plus it is especially frowned upon for divorce attorneys to have sexual relations with their clients. James, I can handle losing my job with my firm here in California, but I cannot handle being disbarred. Do you know what that would mean for me? I won't be able to practice law anywhere else; I'd be finished!"

"I know what it means Celia, just let me think." James got up and began pacing the bare wooden floor that was now devoid of the expensive rugs that he and Elizabeth had acquired over the years.

"You have to do something James," she implored. You still share custody of the kids with her, right? So, that means you both still have a relationship. Please talk to her, convince her to withdraw. I know she hates me and she has all right to, but destroying my life is going too far. Plus, you need to take some responsibility for this too James. If you hadn't shown up at my house that night we wouldn't be in this mess. We had those rules for a reason James, we never meet at our homes, we never book hotel rooms with credit cards, and we never meet close to home, this is all your fault!" Celia shouted at him, bursting into tears, her hands trying tirelessly to swipe her dangling auburn curls from her wet face. James tried to console her by reaching out to hold her but she wouldn't let him touch her.

"My life is ruined too you know," he said in an upset tone, I have no job, I have practically nothing, the life I was used to is now swept from under my feet, I am just as lost as you are."

"You haven't lost everything James," Celia replied angrily. At least you are still a lawyer, she didn't push to have you disbarred, you can join another firm in a heartbeat, but what about me? If she goes through with this I will never be able to work anywhere."

"How long ago did she send you that email?" James asked.

"About three days ago. Why?"

"Just thinking," James answered, "That means she sent you the email before she moved her things from the house yesterday. She has thought this through, and I seriously doubt if I'll have any luck convincing her otherwise. We haven't even decided on the custody schedule as yet so I don't know when I'll even see her. I'm waiting on my lawyer to contact me about the final decision. Celia, I'm really sorry about this, I am, but I can't risk getting further on Elizabeth's bad side. I can't risk losing joint custody of my kids. How do you think she'll take it if I try to talk to her about the welfare of my 'mistress'? I can't promise you anything at least not now, give me some time to get myself together, to work things out regarding my kids and I'll see what can be done, but no promises."

"How did I get here?" Celia muttered under her breath, "from a highly respectable, sought after attorney to the woman who is about to lose it all, and for what? What did I even see in you to risk my career, my reputation?"

"Let's not go down that road," James interjected. "We are both in a sticky situation because of a decision we both consciously made knowing the consequences; so please let's not start pointing fingers, Ok? I said I would try to talk to her but I'm not making any promises, let me just try to get myself together and see what happens over the next couple of weeks. Besides, she has only emailed you, doesn't seem as if she has made any motion against you yet with the courts so let's not jump the gun. Just go home, get some rest, so that you can think straight to try and find a legal way out of this. There must be a way, just go think about it. Talk to some of the attorneys in your circle, and I'll try and reach out to some friends. I'll let you know if I come up with anything and you should do the same."

James kissed Celia on the forehead and walked her to the door. When she left, he couldn't help but blame himself for all that was happening.

What was he to do?

He was at the mercy of Elizabeth, just as Celia was, and on top of that Kayla threatened to make his life a living hell. He felt sorry for Celia, but he had no idea where to start to help her. If Elizabeth had threatened to destroy her, there was nothing he could do, or say now, that would change her mind. He walked over to the broom closet and grabbed the dust bin and went across the room where he had tossed the bourbon bottle, he picked up the larger pieces of broken glass and scooped up the splinters.

As he emptied the dust bin in the kitchen garbage can his phone rang. It was his divorce attorney with the call he had been expecting. "Hey James, its Noel, I have some great news for you, your wife's divorce attorney and I have come to a final decision based on your wife's wishes and the welfare of your kids. If you meet me at my office at noon today, I can fill you in and hand over the documentation you will need regarding the joint custody."

"That sounds great, Noel," James replied. "I will see you at noon, take care now."

Chapter 4

At noon, James hurried to Noel's office. He was anxious to get the details regarding the shared custody of the kids. Noel offered James a seat and proceeded to update him on the final details of the shared custody decision and limitations. "So," said Noel, pushing up his dark, thick-framed eyeglasses from sliding off his nose. "Thank you for meeting with me on such short notice, let's just get straight into why we are here. As was decided, your wife agreed to share custody of the kids—with some reservations and limitations."

James sighed deeply, his face a mask of resignation, He spread his hands. "Go on."

"Well, based on the welfare of the kids, I have accepted the custody agreement on your behalf, as it is the best option you have now if you want a chance to remain in your children's lives, I know some of these options will be less than favorable but allow me to give you all the details before any questions."

James shifted uncomfortably in his seat as he waited for Noel to finish drinking from what looked oddly like a sippy cup.

A knife turned sharply in his chest as scenes from his kids' toddler years flashed across his mind. He braced himself for what was to come.

Noel carefully placed the cup back in its holder on the desk. "So," he cleared his throat. "Firstly, you will share custody with your wife and she gets to choose the dates that she will hand over the kids to you. I have pushed for you to have the children as equally as she will, however she will decide on the exact dates. Secondly, the time spent with your children on the dates your wife decides will be supervised, supervision will only be suspended on the contingency that you secure employment within three months from the day your first custody date begins."

James' jaw dropped, his mouth shaped in an "O". He breathed deeply. He would try to remain calm until Noel concluded.

"Lastly," Noel said in a resolute voice. "Your wife has brought forward that you have a history of abandoning or neglecting your children whenever you start seeing someone new or 'cheating' as she puts it. She has voiced through her attorney that she is concerned that if you start dating or get someone new in your life you may fail to maintain a secure relationship with the children."

Color flooded James' face and Noel raised his forefinger in the air so he could continue. "And, on those grounds, she is requesting that you focus on building and or rebuilding the relationship with your children before considering dating again".

"Bullshit!" James blurted out, he couldn't contain his anger anymore. "She knows my kids are my life, how can she even think that or say that I would abandon or neglect my children for a relationship, and how could you have agreed to something like that, it's ludicrous."

"I didn't agree to that James" Noel interjected. "If you had allowed me to finish I was going to say that I refuted that request under the grounds of an unreasonable compromise. I have proposed to your wife's lawyer that she withdraws that request as it can be detrimental to her custody case as well if we decide to argue a case to the judge that she really doesn't care about your children's well-being but is rather using them to hurt you because her resentment for you."

"That's exactly what she is doing" James responded agitated. He closed his eyes and intake deeply before slowly letting out his breath. Calmer now, he directed his gaze at Noel. His voice steady and deliberate. "She is using our children to get back at me, requesting I agree to all these limitations and conditions in order for me to have shared custody of my children is callous to say the least." He sat back in his chair at a loss. As if he was alone in the room, he whispered out loud, "Elizabeth you have really outdone yourself. How far will you go and what are you trying to prove?"

"Look," Noel said redirecting James attention, "I know all of this is a lot to take in and custody battles are normally painful for both parties especially right after a divorce. What I want you to understand is that she is the favored parent at the moment and any judge will agree with me. In the court's eyes, you are the parent whose actions broke the marriage and you are the parent without a steady stream of income at the moment. This will all work against you if you don't agree to these terms." He paused and peered over his glasses to gauge James' reaction.

James looked back, but not really seeing him. Only the words '. . .if you don't agree to these terms' ricocheting in his head.

"With that said, some of the terms are unreasonable." Noel leaned forward, his tone turned conspiratorial. "Look at the one that suggests control over your date life, I assure you that has been refuted. So, for now, your course of action should be to sign these custody papers agreeing on the rest of the conditions and move forward with the approved communication routes with your wife so that you can be with your children as soon as possible."

Noel handed James the documents and showed him where to sign. He also gave James a schedule showing the suggested timelines that Elizabeth would be available to discuss the visitation schedule. Pursing his lips, James signed the papers with much reservation. His heart splintered at the thought of someone supervising his time spent with his children for God knows how long. He slid the documents back to Noel after he signed and got up from his seat.

Noel gave him a sympathetic glance. "Well then, that will be all. It was a pleasure working with you, please know I'll be here for you whenever you need me, and I will contact you should there be any changes to the agreement. If you have any concerns after today or should your wife violate any of the terms agreed here today, please reach out to me, all the best.

"I will" James responded. They shook hands. "And thank you for everything. I'll keep in touch," James said as he walked out Noel's office.

As James entered the elevator, he took out his phone, punched in the 4-digit code to unlock it and dialed Elizabeth's number. No answer, the call went straight to voicemail. He tried again. Voicemail. Perhaps he would wait until he reached the car to try again.

He was so agitated from everything he had heard in the custody meeting with Noel, he just wanted to confront Elizabeth about it and frankly tell her a piece of his mind. Finally outside, he called her several more times. Still no answer. He knew she was deliberately ignoring his calls and after about the fifth attempt, he slid his phone back into his pocket and walked towards his car.

He was angry and frustrated, he couldn't believe that Elizabeth would try to control his relationship with his kids. And to top it all off she was even trying to control his personal life. The thought of it made him burn with fury inside. He sat in his car, processing her demands. He tried calling her again but still no answer. He started the ignition and without thinking of where he was headed he sped out of the parking lot. James drove for about an hour, with the radio blasting a relic from the old rock group, 'Grateful Dead'. The lead singer screamed:

> *Look, look, at me...what, what, what do you see? You see a broken heart. My baby's bout to set me free...I got tears...tears...and I got pain...pain...pain in my heart....*

James screeched along at the top of his voice, the breeze whipping it into a frenzied echo as he sped down the open road. The song faded out with the guitar strumming, resounding in the far recesses of his heart. He slowed the car and pulled over in a remote area—a short walk away from a secluded beach. He rolled up the foot of his pants, removed his shoes, and just walked along the shoreline kicking at the sand. He couldn't help but think how he had made a mess of things and for what, a piece of ass?

He knew it hadn't gotten to that but the thought of losing his kids made him cringe and a staking pain ran across his heart. He walked away from the water and sat down on a sawed-off tree stump. He had a lot of decisions to make. His toe doodled in the sand. First, he needed a job quickly if he wanted to get unsupervised custody of his kids. Second, he needed to help Celia out of her situation as he shared some of the guilt for what was happening to her, and third, he needed to find a way to speak to Kayla, all of which seemed somewhat difficult from his side of the spectrum.

By now, he slid down to the sand and leaned against the stump. The hours rolled by as he thought about the last time he held his son David in his arms and of the last time he read a bedtime story to his daughter Charlotte. Just by thinking about them he realized that he had missed out on so much with them during the last year when things got rocky with Elizabeth. He pulled his wallet from his back pocket and pulled out a photo with David and Charlotte, as he looked at it he broke down. With tears running down his face he pulled his phone out and called his mom. "Mom" he said as she answered the phone. "I'm just calling to check on the kids are they with you? Can you put them on the phone?"

"Oh honey" Cathy replied, "They are with their mom sweetheart, Charlotte had a violin recital this afternoon and after we got back Elizabeth took them both to celebrate Charlotte's performance. I thought you would have been there but when I asked Elizabeth, she said you had other engagements with your lawyer. It's been over a week now since I've seen you James, I know you must be devastated that it had to come to a divorce, how are you holding up? You need to come by, we need to talk."

"I'm holding up mom, I'll come by tomorrow," James replied.

"I don't think you can come by tomorrow," Cathy's voice held a cautionary note. "Elizabeth is going to bring the kids back tonight and they will be with me until Saturday when she'll move them in with her at the new house. Until you and Elizabeth discuss the arrangements regarding your time with the kids I don't think you can visit them. I'm sorry honey but you know I'm very involved with the affairs of my grandkids and that's what the judge decided. I don't want you to violate that and jeopardize your shared custody of the kids."

"It's ok mom," James interjected. "I know what the judge decided, I was at the custody hearing remember? Anyway, I spoke with my lawyer today and based on the schedule he handed over, I should be meeting with Elizabeth next Monday to discuss the way forward. I'll see you on Sunday then, is that ok?"

" That's fine honey," Cathy replied. "I'll make dinner just bring a bottle of wine, and in case I forget, pick up some dessert too … I love you sweetheart … ."

"Sure mom, I'll do that, and I love you too, see you Sunday."

James hung up, got up and made his way back to his car. It was already getting dark so he headed home. He had decided, then and there, that he had to do whatever it would take for the next couple of days to land a job. There was no way he was going to settle on a supervised custody—not even for a few days. Since securing a job was the only way to ensure that, he knew he had to work hard and fast to secure one. He wanted to at least have a few prospects before his first visit with the kids. However, he knew things could get difficult. During the time he headed Elizabeth's late dad's firms and businesses, he had become a well-known lawyer and powerful businessman, he wasn't naïve to the fact that the reason behind the sudden loss of this power would be the topic on everyone's tongue. He was afraid of the ridicule that he might face going in front of these people to grovel for a job. Starting his own firm was still a possibility but that would take time, so for now, he had to swallow his pride and do what was necessary to save the relationship with his kids.

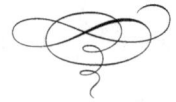

Chapter 5

At the office, Kayla sat at her desk and stared at the view outside. Although she was looking she wasn't really seeing much as she mulled over the week's events. She was trying hard to convince herself that James really didn't love her and that he had only used her, but she couldn't help but think about what Liz had said.

Did he really fall in love with her?

Did he end the relationship with her because Liz gave him no choice?

What had really transpired between him and Liz that drove him to Vancouver? The more she thought about it, she couldn't quite understand why a devoted husband would travel for a business trip and turn it into a love hunt where he ended up being in a relationship with someone else besides his wife for so many years. If everything was peachy at home, it was either he was bent on deceiving her into loving him for all those years or there was more to the story that Liz did not tell her; Not that any of it would have made any difference, because she knew the entire ordeal with James should never have happened in the first place.

The sound of her phone ringing snapped her out of her thoughts. She reached for her phone and noticed that it was Liz calling. "Hey babe" she answered,

"Just checking in on you," Liz responded on the other end of the line sounding quite happy and cheery. "So…" Liz continued, "I was thinking that since I'll be off from work for a little while until the kids are settled and comfortable with the custody arrangements and new schedules between their dad and I, perhaps we could use this time to bond with the kids? I would love for you to consider staying with us for a while just so the kids can meet you formally and, also, I think it will help them to come to terms with our relationship. They'll be moving in on Saturday and I was thinking you could come stay with us the following week; what do you think?"

If Liz was able to see the expression on Kayla's face at the sound of that question, she would know immediately what she was thinking. Quite frankly, she wasn't ready to move in with Liz, she wanted to but she didn't think this was the right time. The silence on Kayla's end prompted Liz to ask the question again. "So, what do you think?"

" I think it is a good idea Liz", Kayla answered quickly. "I just don't think now is the right time though, I mean, don't you think you should first sort out the arrangement with James and the kids, get them to feel comfortable with that aspect of this situation first before formally bringing me into the picture? I may be wrong, but I think it will be too much for them to handle all at once. You know, dealing with our relationship and the changes in their relationship with their dad." With the deafening silence, sweat began to form tiny beads and pucker Kayla's upper lip. She clutched the phone tightly to her ear as if trying to hear something…anything from Liz. She rushed on in a deflated breath. "If anything, Liz, I think we should ease them into the status of our relationship over time. A big step, like me moving in, as soon as their dad is out, might not be a good idea." Silence. "Liz are you still there?"

"Yes, I am, and I totally agree with you."

Kayla breathed easier. She didn't realize how tense she was.

"I guess I was so excited by the thought of having us all together that I didn't take time to think it through," Liz said. "I tell you what, how about dinner Sunday evening with us? She gushed. "It could kick start the process of easing them into our relationship and would give them an opportunity to get to know you a bit better."

"That sounds perfect," Kayla replied with a smile in her voice. "And since they won't be moving in until Saturday, how about we use the rest of this week to have our own little rendezvous?"

"Oooh, I like the sound of that," Liz smacked her lips in satisfaction. So, see you tomorrow then?"

"Yeah, I'll drop by on my way from work." Kayla's sultry tone hinted of more than a "drop by."

After they hung up, Liz went back to putting the finishing touches to her son David's room. She arranged a few of his favorite stuff toys on the bed then stood in the corner of the room, at a distance, to take it all in. Glancing around the room she knew something was missing but she couldn't pinpoint what it was. She untied the window curtains, turned off the lights and left the room. Along the hallway walking from David's room she popped into the room she had also set up for her daughter Charlotte, everything was perfect. She had a good feeling of accomplishment and headed for the kitchen.

She opened the refrigerator and glanced around. "I need to go shopping tomorrow," she murmured, staring at the almost bare refrigerator shelves. Opening the freezer, she found the last packaged dinner. "Pasta with meat sauce it is." She brandished it in the air, trying to sound excited like they do on the *Food Network* shows. She shoved it into the microwave, and as she waited for the five-minute countdown, she remembered. "The rocking pony!" she shouted, "That's what's missing from David's room. I knew I forgot something, it's in the basement at the other house." She caught herself, she was babbling like she did as a child with her imaginary friends. Should she call James to bring over the rocking pony? Nah, she didn't really want to talk to him at this moment, she was in too much of a good mood. She looked at her watch, it was a quarter to seven, it's already late. Tomorrow, she would go over and get it...tomorrow.

At the beep of the microwave, Liz pulled the dish out and scooped the contents onto a plate. She poured herself a glass of red wine and headed to the living room with her meal. She sat on the couch facing the television, turned it on and then scrolled through Netflix to find a movie that could hold her over for the rest of the evening.

That evening when James got home he delved right into networking with some of his lawyer friends, firms and acquaintances. He sent a few emails notifying some firms of his interest.

After some time had passed, he grabbed a beer from the refrigerator and sat at the kitchen counter just sipping and scrolling through his phone. Without even knowing he was doing it, his mind went rogue, scanning memories with Kayla. He thought about how great she was and how he had really fallen for her. He felt bad about hurting her the way he did. His mind created scenarios of what would happen if he could get a chance to speak to her alone now, to explain all that had happened and why he had to do what he did. She would probably see that he is really not a bad person and that his intention was not to deceive and abandon her.

Before he knew it, he had finished the bottle of beer. He was at the fridge door to get another when he decided that was not how he wanted to spend the night. He went upstairs, undressed and had a shower. After showering, James selected his favorite playlist on his iPod, docked it and went straight to bed, with hopes that he would have some job prospects in the morning from the networking he did earlier on.

Kayla left the office late that evening, she got home around 10 pm; she had a client dinner meeting at seven that same evening which ended a little after eight. When she got in, she quickly kicked off her heels and undressed and headed for the shower. She took her time in the warm water soothing her aching shoulders and feet. After her shower, she wrapped herself in a towel as she walked around her bedroom toweling her wet hair. She stood in front of the mirror and just stared at herself for a while. Some months ago, she was beginning to feel confident that things were beginning to look up for her in her love life. Some weeks ago, she was sure she had found the one to fill the empty hole James had left in her heart. And, some days ago, she was ready to take a big leap of faith and give herself completely to someone else.

But now she was questioning everything.

It's not that she didn't love Liz, but she would be lying to herself if she didn't admit that seeing James again and learning that he had truly loved her, despite his less than honest way of getting her to fall for him awoke some feelings that she just couldn't deny. She pulled her now dry hair up in a ponytail and applied some body butter to her damp skin. Dropping the towel that had wrapped her body at the side of her bed, she snuggled up under her blanket, lapping one of the pillows between her legs. She picked up her phone and looked at the time, it was now minutes to midnight. She sent Liz a quick text message, "Had a late work dinner meeting, got home some minutes ago, going to bed now. Miss you and see you tomorrow for dinner. Sweet dreams :)".

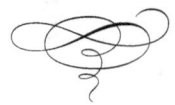

Chapter 6

Liz saw Kayla's message around 4 am the next day, when she woke up and checked her phone. The smiley face at the end of Kayla's message made her smile. She responded with a smiley face and a short text, "Just got your message, can't wait to see you later today, I'm up to an early start as I have some errands to run. Love you."

Liz rolled out of bed and got herself ready for a run, she pulled out of the driveway with the intention of dropping by James first to get Daniel's rocking pony. From experience, she assumed James would be out for his 5 am run by the time she'd get there. She would just let herself in with her key, grab the pony and leave, that way she wouldn't need to see or exchange words with him until she had to. He wouldn't even know that she stopped by. She preferred it that way.

About thirty minutes later she pulled up in the driveway of her old home, she grabbed the house keys from the glove compartment and let herself in through the front door. The minute she walked in her eyes went straight to the misplaced chair cushions, the glass rings formed on her glass coffee table because James did not use a coaster, and her table centerpiece that was now pushed about thirty degrees out from the center of the table. She tried to ignore it but her OCD wouldn't let her. She spent about two minutes putting everything back in its place, before she went upstairs to the bedroom. She slightly pushed the door open and when she saw that James wasn't in bed she went in.

She looked around the room and there were so many things out of place to drive her insane. "Liz you are here to get Daniel's rocking pony" She grumbled. "Just get it and go and stop fixating on the things that are out of place." She open the top drawer of her bedside table and took out a key. She turned to walk out of the room but was startled upon hearing, "Liz, what are you doing here?"

She slowly turned around to see James coming from the bathroom, wrapped in a towel from the waist down. "What are you doing here Liz?" He asked again, his voice barely containing his fury.

"I thought you would be out running," she responded, staring at his bare chest sheepishly. "Anyways," she said, tossing back her head defiantly and locking eyes with him. "I thought I'd swing by to get Daniel's rocking pony. Her eyes challenged him. "I noticed I didn't have it when I was setting up his new room, you know how much he loves that thing so I just thought I'd come get it early when you were out for your morning run so I wouldn't have to bother you."

"Bother me," he said, looking at her, with a curl of disdain on his lips. "You didn't come here early so you wouldn't have to bother me. You came here early so you wouldn't have to see me, you have been ignoring my calls for days now, and you know damn well that I have a lot that I want to say to you." His eyes seemed to bore through hers, his voice rising with suppressed anger. He took a step closer and wagged his finger at her. "Especially about that stunt you pulled regarding the custody agreements." She could see he was boiling inside. He stepped away from her and grabbed a T-shirt from the closet and slipped it over his head.

As he shrugged the shirt over his wide shoulders he chastised her. "You have some damn nerves barging in here after ignoring all my calls. I'm a lot of things Elizabeth, but I'm not a bad father. How could you stipulate such ridiculous contingencies of what you think will make me fit to have unsupervised visits with my own children? You ruin my life, my career and then demand that I need to have a job before I can have the kids on my own? And, as if that's not bad enough you move on with someone else but try to control my love life. Good God! You even suggest to the lawyers that I might abandon or neglect my children if I start dating again. Damn! How callous can you be Elizabeth!"

"I ruined your life and your career?" Liz asked rhetorically. "The last time I checked you did that all on your own because you couldn't keep your dick in your pants. I only suggested to my lawyer that it is in the best interest of our children if you focus on rebuilding your relationship with them before considering dating again. We both know that your dick takes over your rationality and logics once you start getting some and you pay little or no attention to anything or anyone else around you."

James threw up his hand in the air, in disgust, as if pleading for deliverance from a higher power.

"You want to talk about callous James, let's talk about how you were sleeping with our family lawyer right under my nose, and at the same time fucking my psychologist a woman I poured my heart out to. She knew the most intimate details of our relationship. She watched me cry every Friday, at 1 pm, in her office for the past year. She advised and comforted me while secretly laughing at how pathetic I was because she was screwing my husband. God knows how many other women are out there ridiculing me behind my back, because my dear husband decided to make a spectacle of me by making his dick free for all!"

The look on James face told Liz that he was surprised she knew about his fling with their psychologist, and she capitalized on his sudden silence. "You didn't know I knew about her, did you?" she laughed without mirth. "Took me a while to find out but I did, wished I had found out sooner too because I wouldn't have spent all my money on those good for nothing sessions. I found out the week we were finalizing our divorce. I saw the emails on your work laptop when I was clearing out your office. You know what puzzles me though James? She asked, while walking circles around him. "Why you made it your mission to screw all the women that I knew, the women who knew my vulnerabilities, who knew intimate details about us. Why? You son-of-a-gun!" Unwittingly, the hot tears flowed down her cheeks.

"Isn't it obvious?" James responded, walking out of her hypnotic circle dance around him. He looked at her warily as if she was a black widow spider weaving an intricate web to entrap him to his doom. "You blame me for my infidelity but you fail to take responsibility for the reasons I became unfaithful. You stand here shedding tears, playing the victim, but Elizabeth you are not the innocent victim in all of this. When I got married to you, I did so because I loved you with every fiber in me, at least the version of you I knew back in law school. But the minute I said, "I do," the real Elizabeth emerged. You changed, and you know it! You became a control freak, making me into the version of me that you had in your head. You sabotaged all my efforts to start my own practice, and why? Because a civil litigation lawyer was not the husband my dear Elizabeth wanted to be married to."

She stopped in her tracks, her jaw dropped. Shell-shocked; her eyes were without remorse .

He was on a roll. "You knew my dreams from law school, so why marry me if you didn't like who I wanted to become? Let me answer that for you, because I was just a project for you, a fixer-upper; another "blank slate" that you wanted to mold into your perfect man. You forced me into working for your dad's company, when you were in a position to step in and run it yourself. But you wouldn't have that, would you? Because social status and what everyone else thinks of you, matters more to you than my happiness. How dare the husband of a socialite, over-privileged, power-stricken, wealthy heiress, consider working his way up to the top? He asked in a malignant tone like splintered gall.

She continued to stare at him surprised at his tone but still without remorse.

His eyes glazed over with memory as he ranted. "My dear wife squirmed at the thought of being married to a struggling civil litigation lawyer. You know what you said to me when I started searching for office space for my firm? Let me refresh your memory my dear wife."

No one knows you James, it will take years for you to become a respected lawyer in this state, years before the status of your firm will ever come close to the status and reputation of my family's firms and companies.

Why start from the bottom when you can start at the top?

Why start from nothing when you can have everything?

My reputation is everything to me James, my husband should be a man of status, class, and power and that is what you will have if you take over my family's firms. People know me James, they know my father. I will have controlling stake in my dad's firm and companies regardless if I run it or not.

But as for you, we need to make your name.

We need to build your status and there's no better way to do so than heading one of the most powerful and respected firms in this state.

"That's what you said to me Elizabeth! and that stayed with me till this very day. I knew you were changing but when you said that to me, I knew my dreams and happiness didn't matter to you. You didn't love me. You loved the idea of what you could make me into. You wanted me in a position where you would always have the upper-hand, where you could control me and that's exactly what you spent the rest of our marriage doing, controlling me, making me into your image of power, class and stature."

A sound escaped Elizabeth's lips much like the squawk of a shocked bird being pounced on by a swooping, predatory vulture. But she quickly held her ground.

On cue, he flapped his arms, raising his elbows high in the air to wriggle and get comfortable in his too-tight T-shirt. "And don't even get me started on our love life," he continued. "We used to be all over each other back in law school, but after marriage we only had sex when you said it was ok. Or, if it fit into your perfect schedule. For God's sake, Elizabeth, we only had sex when you were ovulating! That's what...once a month? Sex in our marriage was only for procreation and when Charlotte came we didn't even have sex at all! I waited for you, I was patient, and I thought you needed time to get back to yourself after Charlotte, but that didn't happen. You pushed me away Elizabeth! The last time I spoke to you about our sex life, you practically told me that there was more important things to direct my focus and energy on, like making sure that your father's firms remained on top of the competition and building on his legacy."

"Not fair, not fair at all...."

He cut her off in mid-sentence and continued spilling his vitriol. "Our marriage was crash landing before I cheated and you know it. You want to know why I fell in love with Kayla? Because she was everything you were when I first met you. She loved me for me. Her love for me was pure. It didn't matter... class and status. What I lost with you I found in her and I was hooked, because I yearned for that Elizabeth, and that's why my relationship with her lasted so long."

Elizabeth cackled in dawning realization. She knew what the son-of-a-bitch was trying to do. Divide and conquer. He would like to have her turn on Kayla now, to breed seeds of discontent between them. But, there was no stopping the bastard in his tirade as he continued spewing his guts.

"When you found out about Kayla, I came clean and told you why I cheated. I was honest as to why I fell in love with her, and you took some of the responsibility then, and promised that you would change, but after David you went right back to your old self. And that's why I never broke things off with Kayla. I kept her close because I knew you wouldn't keep your word."

She shook her head, from side-to-side, bestowing him with a pitying gaze as if he had just escaped from Bedlam.

He sneered at her, his face a mask of disgust. "But leave it up to you to crush any glimmer of happiness in my life, you made it your mission to make my life miserable, you made it so I had no choice but to end things with her permanently and in all that you still wouldn't change or even try to give me a fraction of the happiness that you were taking from me." He stopped pacing, and sat at the foot of his bed, his hands resting on his knees. In a self-righteous, 'I am the victim voice' he continued. "When I destroyed my relationship with Kayla, I slept with those other women, especially women you knew, not because I had feelings for them," he laughed deep in his chest. "It's because it gave me joy...you hear me? Joy!" He used one hand to pound his chest. "Yes, deep down inside, I felt joy, to know that I was somehow tarnishing that perfect image that you cared so much about. That image you valued more than your husband, it brought me joy that people would look at you and know that this facade, this charade of a marriage that you portray to everyone else as perfect was not so perfect, and my dear wife it felt good."

James looked at her with a glimmer of satisfaction in his eyes, breathing hard, and trying to catch a breath after all that he had said. He rose from his seat and strode towards the door, indicating that he was done, but Liz stopped him with an imperial flick of her wrist.

She studied him as bile rose in her throat. "All I ever did was to set you up for success," she said. "The way I went about it might not have been perfect, but if I was to make you into the man you were meant to be, it meant lots of sacrifice, discipline and hard work. Marriage is not all about sex James! we had our entire lives ahead of us to have pointless sex and real happiness, once you had achieved all you needed to achieve but you were impatient."

It was his turn to look at her with pity. After all this, the bitch still didn't get it.

"You've had your say and you will listen to me now." She pursed her lips in determination. "I watched my mother groom and mold my father into the man that he became, she made sure he was focused and dedicated to creating a legacy for his family and that is the man who built an empire from the ground up. If I was going to ensure that their legacy extended to my children, I had to make sure that my husband shared the same vision and would stop at nothing to ensure the same. My father didn't get where he was, slacking and thinking small, he made sacrifices and it was hard work. But you, my dear husband, are a dreamer. You never looked at the bigger picture, you would settle at being good when we could be great. You needed someone to push you to be great and that's exactly what I did."

She ignored his loud, exhaled swoosh of a breath and went right on talking. "However, you decided that you didn't want to be great, you fought all my efforts with your petty complaints and cheating escapades.

So, I decided to give you what you fought so tirelessly for, NOTHING; because without me you are nothing."

James opened and closed his mouth like a fish. "Call it what you will James, but ever since law school I aimed high, I made it clear to you that I was the successor of my parents' legacy so you knew what you were getting yourself into when you asked me to marry you. Your dreams, James, were mediocre. I made you into a coveted man that all your peers wanted to be like. I gave you a life that most men only dreamed about. Luxury condos at your disposal in over twelve states, lake houses and private cabins in the most exotic countries in the world, powerful alliances on your payroll, the head of one of the most reputable firms in the world, two beautiful children and wealth beyond your wildest dreams. And, you stand here talking about sex and happiness? James you are pathetic...."

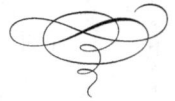

Chapter 7

Liz pushed passed James who was standing at the bedroom door. She stormed downstairs and James followed behind her. "I never married you for wealth and status Elizabeth," he said. 'I married you for love, and since you had forgotten what it meant to love someone I went and found it with someone else." He breathed hard and rapid as he hurried after her.

At the foot of the stairs, she stopped with a swift pivot on her heels. She rested her hands on both hips, while one foot tapped the floor. He seemed relieved not to be speaking to her back. "Elizabeth, in all this," he said, gesturing with wide open arms. "I never once neglected my children and you know it. In the past year when I made them spend more time with my mom, it wasn't because I was neglecting them. It was because I didn't want them to get consumed in the toxic aftermath of our constant fighting and indifference. With all the crazy, despicable and overbearing things you did, I never once questioned your love for our children and you should not question mine." He mirrored her stance with his hands on his hips. He leaned forward to peer in her face, his voice low.

"Have you stopped to ask yourself what you stand to gain from all this?

Have you even considered what this divorce will do to our children?" His lips curled into a snarl, baring his teeth. Elizabeth blinked hard to dispel the notion of fangs. His voice turned sharp and biting: "Your despicable ways may have pushed me into the arms of other women, but I never once considered divorcing you. Instead, I found ways to cope so that I wouldn't have to hurt my kids, so I wouldn't have to turn their world upside down, at least not while they are so young."

Elizabeth rolled her eyes and sighed heavily.

"You can roll your eyes all you want, but I bet you didn't consider that did you? You opted for a divorce every chance you got, and despite the hell of a marriage I was living in with you, I was always the one fighting to keep us together." He chuckled under his breath. "Not for your sake, but for Charlotte and David. I figured out a long time ago that as long as you are in control, you consider yourself to be winning and nothing else matters, because we are all damn pawns in your game of chess." Dawning realization flooded his eyes. He folded his arms across his chest as if a chill wind entered the room. "Which leads me to my questions," he all but whispered it.

"Is Kayla just another pawn?

Is she your winning move, to, as you put it, leave me with nothing?

Is that what your so-called relationship is all about?"

He circled her, slowly wagging his finger at her. "I know what you are capable of Elizabeth, because I have seen and lived it firsthand, I don't believe that the universe just happened to shift in your favor and direct Kayla of all people into your life. A woman you vowed to inflict your wrath on if you ever came face-to-face with her. What is going on Elizabeth. Why is Kayla in California?"

"This conversation is over!" Elizabeth shouted as she fiddled with the keys to open the door to the basement.

"It is far from over," James said, grabbing onto her hand and blocking her from opening the basement door. "I know you are up to something Elizabeth and God help you if it is what I think it is."

"I don't know what you are talking about James, it was total coincidence that I met Kayla. I met her at WhisPer, and I was drawn to her from the moment she walked in. I saw power, status and class dripping from her, that's why I pursued her and that's the truth."

"I don't believe that for a second," James responded. "Don't forget, Elizabeth, I've been married to you for almost a decade, I know you too well to know that you have the resources and the connections to get whatever it is you want. What I don't understand is why Kayla would be with you if she knows that you are, or were, my wife."

"Be careful you don't burst a blood vessel trying to figure out what doesn't concern you James. All you need to know is that Kayla and I love each other. From the moment she realized that you were my husband, her Jay, she told me everything you did to her, not that I hadn't already known. I must admit, I felt pity hearing it from her own mouth. I'll admit one thing to you James, I do understand why you fell in love with her; she's sophisticated, honest, and a powerful woman—the woman manages wealth for crying out loud, much like myself. I won't need to change her James, because she's already everything I tried to make you into."

James visibly winced at her words. Every word Elizabeth uttered seemed to dig the stake a little deeper into his chest. He leaned back against the wall, his head thrown back in resignation as he listened.

"When I got married to you James," She continued as she stepped closer to get him to look in her eyes. "I couldn't avoid the unfortunate case of taking your last name, and that meant that if I had allowed you to pursue your silly little dreams of owning a corner office law firm begging for clients, I too would be consumed and stained with your failure because I bore your name. So, I did everything in my power to ensure that you become your best you, but you couldn't see the bigger picture. I knew it was a matter of time before I had to let you go, I wouldn't let you tarnish my reputation, no longer than you already had, knowing your track record with these whores."

James raised his hand in the air, with his palm up, as if he had enough. But, she had to have her catharsis. His eyes looked hunted and his glance rested longingly on the window as if a way to escape her tirade.

Elizabeth's face seemed less tight as the words flowed from her mouth. She threw him a self-satisfied look as she berated him. "I knew that if and when I had divorced you, you wouldn't have any claims on my family's wealth and legacy, but knowing you, I knew that wouldn't have mattered much, because you'd just run back to your mediocre career dream. If I was to truly leave you with nothing that meant hitting you where I knew it would hurt the most, crushing your heart. You see, I knew you would eventually go searching for her, because once you love someone your love runs deep and that's your greatest weakness."

"So, I was right all along," James said, moving away from the basement door, your meeting Kayla was no coincidence." He jabbed a finger at her, "You! parading Kayla as your new love is solely to hurt me. Jesus Christ Elizabeth! I knew after a year into our marriage that you were crazy, but this is a new level of crazy. You will stop at nothing to get what you want, will you! Kayla has done nothing wrong. Why drag her into this. Have you even been honest with her at all? Why am I even asking you that, you are the master of deception, playing games, toying with people's emotions, playing the victim. I bet she thinks that once again I'm the bad guy, the sole reason for our divorce." He rubbed his hands together as if there was a chill in the air. "So, what's the plan Elizabeth, make her fall in love with you? Sabotage her career? Push her off a cliff?" Elizabeth's eyes widened at the latter. "And to what end, to make me suffer?" His breath came out in a long swoosh. "Do you honestly think I'll sit back and watch you destroy her life like you did mine? I'll tell her everything!"

"Tell her what James?" Elizabeth asked heatedly. "Tell her that I'm using her to hurt you! Tell her that us meeting was no coincidence? And what makes you think that she'll ever believe a word that comes out of your mouth. What makes you think that she'll ever speak to you again?" Her voice rose higher, and she cackled wildly into a semblance of laughter which didn't quite reach her eyes. "You were right James, you are a pawn in my game of chess, you are the weakest piece, my foot soldier, but Kayla is no pawn, at least not anymore. I think she has proven her love and allegiance such that she can be my queen. You are both where I want you to be, I bet if you could do it all over again, you would think twice before you cross me." With that said, Liz seemed visibly calmer. She gave James a smug grin and opened the basement door to go for the rocking pony.

James was dumbstruck by all he had just heard and he was finding it difficult to process the information. All he could think about was what would be Kayla's fate? How would he begin to tell her, if he even had the chance, and would she believe him?

As Liz came back from the basement, holding the rocking pony in her hand, James moved closer to her. "I promise you Elizabeth... he said staring her dead in the eyes, "I will not allow you to hurt her, I will do everything in my power to let her know who you really are."

"And who said I was going to hurt her? Liz responded maliciously. "Lest you forget, James, Kayla and I have one thing in common, we both hate you, and until that change, I will continue to be the fragile, broken ex-wife of deceptive serial liar and cheater James Cassidy. As long as she remains on my side I'll be everything she wants me to be, much like you could have had. So, bear one thing in mind James, if you meddle, if you interfere, in any way, to turn Kayla against me, don't go blaming me for what will become of her and that, my dear ex-husband, is a promise."

His eyes widened in alarm at her veiled threat.

"Now"…She continued, "I suggest you invest your time and efforts into finding a suitable job if you want unsupervised visits with your children. You know I am one for stability, and I won't allow my children to stay with you in a home with no means of providing for them. So, next time we meet, which I believe is on Monday to discuss custody scheduling concerning the welfare of our kids. I hope for your sake that you would have landed a job by then or at least have some prospects to show." Confident in her own power, she bent and pushed the rocking horse playfully across the floor. "Goodbye for now James, I have dinner plans with Kayla later tonight and I want everything to be perfect. Who knows, I might even ask her to marry me," she said, looking at James with a deceptive smile… "I think the Westbrook name would suit her perfectly, don't you think?" She asked, laughing as she walked out the door.

James fell to the coach as if someone had just stabbed him in the heart. He was no innocent towards Kayla, but he was never this callous, he didn't pretend to love her, he really did. How could he warn Kayla without putting her in danger? And how could he live with himself if he did not? The realization hit him like a sledge hammer to the face, Elizabeth had him right where she wanted—and there was nothing he could do about it.

Chapter 8

Liz's tiff with James had derailed her from her intended early morning run. After retrieving David's rocking pony, she instead drove straight to the farmers market to get some fresh herbs and vegetables for her dinner plans with Kayla. As she walked through the market, she glanced at the fresh strawberries, on a stand, and she just couldn't resist. "Were these picked today?" she asked the vendor.

"Yes Mam...," the vendor responded, "fresh from the field to the stand."

Liz smiled at her and took one of the strawberries and bit into it with a satisfying grin on her face. "Fresh indeed," she said in agreement with the vendor. "They'll be perfect for my Pavlova dessert this evening," she smiled. She bought a tray of the strawberries and went to get the remainder of her dinner ingredients.

After leaving the farmers market, she got into her car and made a call. "May I speak to Margo, tell him it's Elizabeth."

"Good morning Mrs. Cassidy," said Margo on the other end of the line.

"It's no longer Cassidy darling its back to Westbrook. I think that suited me better, don't you think?" She asked rhetorically with a shallow laugh. "Well, let's not talk about things of the past Margo, that's not why I'm calling. I need an engagement ring and I need it within the next two hours. I need an emerald-cut diamond, sixty-seven percent in depth, a table percent no lower than seventy, with a slightly thick girdle."

"Excellent choice Miss Westbrook, may I suggest a length to width ratio of about 1.5, preferable rectangular in shape?"

"Oh, you know me so well Margo, she answered with delight. "I will pick it up at around noon."

"Miss Westbrook, a diamond ring with those custom specifics usually takes up to twenty-four hours to perfect, I'm afraid two hours won't be enough. For you, I could have it ready in five hours at best."

"I'll give you three hours Margo, I need that ring tonight and you know I'm not one to take no for an answer. So, I suggest you get to work, see you at 1 pm then, charge it to my credit card, and be sure to compensate yourself for your time.

Liz drove out of the farmers market parking lot, making her way to the local butcher to get fresh cut steak for dinner. She made another call. "It's Elizabeth Westbrook, Gina, I'd like to send a vase of Stargazer Lilies, pinks and reds only, to one Kayla Riviera of DMC Wealth Management on Berkley Towers. A simple note please, 'I miss you…love James' no other information needed.".

"When do you want it delivered?"

"Please have it delivered as early as you can, I have a feeling it will make her day so much better... thank you." She hung up the phone with a pleased smile and turned up the music in her jeep. She slipped on her shades and sped away to perfect her plans for the rest of the evening.

After visiting the butcher and the grocery store, Liz made a final stop at her local winery to pick up a bottle of her favorite wine to have with steak, Cabernet Sauvignon. It was Kayla's favorite too but she already knew that. She was proud of her meticulously planned night with Kayla. As she walked out from the winery to her car she glanced at her watch. It was already a quarter to one. It was perfect timing to stop by Margo her jeweler for the engagement ring. As she was about to enter her car she was intercepted by an old acquaintance, Marcella.

"Oh, Elizabeth darling, it has been months since I've seen you around here."

"Marcella," Liz responded, they greeted each other with kisses from cheek-to-cheek. Marcella and Liz knew each other since high school, their relationship was one hinged mainly on societal status than a friendship based on mutual love and respect for one another. Marcella is the daughter of one Jax Charbay; owner of one of the largest winery and distillery in California. Marcella and Liz spent most of their high school days and adulthood competing with each other. Who could own the most expensive cars and cruise on the most luxurious yacht. Who had the most noteworthy friends and have the wildest and biggest parties.

They acted civil with each other but deep down they hated each other because their obsession with being better than the other had started a rivalry that seemed never ending. Marcella ended up marrying into more wealth... 'For better and for a bigger checkbook', Liz often criticized, not for love. However, Liz knew she was the sole heir to her father's empire so she told herself she didn't need to seek more wealth. She convinced herself that it was better to marry for love. Walking into the country clubs and rubbing shoulders with the likes of Marcella and her husband were some of the reasons she had pushed James into a lifestyle that he didn't much care for.

"Yes, it has been a while," Liz continued. "You know how it is, busy with work and with two kids, I hardly get time to run errands." They smiled at each other with smiles as fake as the relationship they both shared.

"Oh, I heard about the divorce Elizabeth, said Marcella. It's such a shame, I really liked James.

"I'm sure you do," Elizabeth mumbled under her breath maintaining her fake smile.

"I would often see him around here, Marcella continued, mostly because he was the one running the errands..."

"I'd love to stay and chat Marcella," Elizabeth interjected cutting her off. "But I'm running late to a meeting."

"Running late to a meeting in your jogging outfit? Oh, Elizabeth, I'm sure you can come up with more convincing lies to avoid a conversation with me," Marcella said with a derisive grin.

"You'll never change, will you? Elizabeth asked with an annoyed grin. Not all meetings require formal attire. As I said, I'm running late to a meeting, I'll see you around. Take care now and send my regards to your husband, will you?"

She got in her car and drove off. Marcella stood there, with her glamour sunshades on, staring until Liz turned the corner. Liz got to Margo about half an hour later than she had agreed, which was even better for Margo in her mind. She took the elevator up to Margo's private office and showroom. Margo stood behind his showcase waiting for her. He walked out to greet her as soon as she stepped through the door.

"*Bienvenue*, Miss Westwood," Margo said with a peck on Elizabeth's cheek.

"*Je vous remercie*," she responded to Margo, pecking him back on his cheek. "Is it ready?" Elizabeth said, walking over to the sofa to her immediate right.

"Yes, it is," replied Margo, walking to his show case to retrieve a small blood-red box from the top shelf. He walked to Elizabeth who was now seated on the couch and sat beside her. He handed her the box with much anticipation in his eyes. "I'm confident you will find everything to your liking as you have requested." Elizabeth glanced at him with a slightly raised left eyebrow and opened the box.

"I have faith in you Margo," she said, staring at the perfection in the box, sparkling back at her. "It's just as I expected it to be...flawless." Her voice was filled with awe.

Margo beamed at her compliments.

Elizabeth continued in a soft tone. "She'll have no choice than to love it."

"I'm sure whoever it will be presented to will appreciate its magnificence," Margo replied with much relief in his voice.

"I'll be taking my leave now," Elizabeth said, getting up from the couch.

"Always a pleasure doing business with you Miss Westbrook, I'm happy we can once again meet and exceed your expectations."

Elizabeth nodded in agreement and Margo walked with her to the door.

"*Jusqu'à ce qu'on se revoie,*" Margo said as the elevator door closed.

At DMC, Kayla walked to her office after a board meeting with the managing partners of her firm. She was mostly working out of the office today, meeting with one client after the next at their preferred locations. Her board meeting that started since 12'oclock had now ended at a quarter to two. As she walked into her office, she noticed the vase of Stargazer Lilies on her desk. The fact that the lilies were her favorite and in her preferred colors made her smile. Liz, she thought, but how could she have known? She couldn't remember discussing the topic of her favorite flowers with her. She however knew that Liz had her ways of figuring things out about her. Liz had surprised her quite a few times with some information she had never disclosed to her, and so she was sticking with that guess.

She placed her bag and her tablet on her desk, opened her blinds to let some natural light in and then she attended to the flowers. She noticed the small envelope in the middle of the bouquet on a card holder. She detached the envelope, sat down and removed the small card inside. Her eyes darted immediately to the words "...*Love James.*" It was a small note with just five words, so of course she read it in one glance, but the two words that stood out the most were "...*Love James.*"

She suddenly felt a bit warm and uncomfortable.

How did he know where she worked?

Why would he send her flowers after all that has happened?

What games was he playing?

The questions flooded her mind, and she didn't know if she really needed to know the answers. She slid the note under the keyboard of her computer and dialed the extension for front desk.

"Good afternoon Miss Riviera, how may I be of service?"

"Good afternoon Victor," she responded. "Did you sign for some flowers for me this afternoon?"

"Yes, Miss Riviera I did, they actually arrived at 10 am this morning. However, I knew you were not scheduled for the office until the afternoon so I had them sent up pending your arrival. Is there something wrong?"

"No Victor, nothing wrong" Kayla answered absently while her mind teemed with questions. "I just want to know who delivered them…..."

"They were delivered by courier Miss Riviera," Victor responded. "CCS courier services to be exact. No sender name/company on the courier receipt I signed.

"Thank you, Victor," she responded, with a slight disappointment in her voice. "That will be all," and she hung up.

She didn't want to think much about it, but it wasn't as if she could help it; the question why was still bugging her. What did he hope to accomplish by sending her flowers? and her favorite lilies too. The nerve of him to pull that stunt. It made her blood boil a bit. She picked up her phone and called her assistant Lisa into her office.

"Could you discard these please? She asked Lisa, pointing to the vase of lilies.

"Are you sure?" Lisa responded, hesitantly lifting the vase.

"You may do whatever you want with them Lisa," Kayla said in a disgruntled tone. "Take them home, give them to someone, whatever you want...That will be all, she said curtly. She turned her attention to her computer. Lisa took the vase of lilies and exited her office.

When Liz got home she went straight into prepping dinner, she had the steak prepped and partially cooked on the stove top and was finished by 4:30 pm. The *Pavlova* was done and set on a cake tray on the table. A fresh spring salad topped with freshly grated parmesan cheese and Italian seasoned croutons was the final addition to her perfectly set table. The wine was in the wine cooler chilling, candles were lit and set at an angle on the table and strategically placed around the room. Music played softly in the background.

Based on Kayla's text message earlier on in the afternoon, she would be heading home from work around 6 pm and would be here for dinner by 8 pm Liz got out of the shower around 7:15 pm. She sat in front of her mirror, applied body butter to her body and did her makeup. She removed the towel from her hair and lightly brushed it over and over for about ten minutes. She walked to her bed where she had a dress laid out, simple, yet elegant semi-casual, and it hugged her frame in all the right places. It was in a beautiful scarlet color that complemented her hair and her glacier blue eyes. She slipped into the dress, zipped it from the side and she stood in front of the mirror pleased with herself. The finishing touch, a dab of Coco Chanel's, *Mademoiselle* perfume. Her perfectly planned night was about to begin.

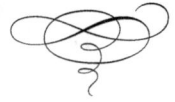

Chapter 9

At the sound of the doorbell, Liz made her way down the stairs. "I need to get you a key," she said as she opened the door to let Kayla in. They smiled at each other and Liz gave Kayla a peck on the cheek.

"Love the dress...," Kayla said admiring Liz's attire. "Seems I'm a bit underdressed," Kayla joked.

"Oh, don't be silly, Liz said as a flush of color swept up her cheeks. "I haven't worn this dress in a while and I just thought I'd put it on for you. And, you look stunning as always." With a wave of her hand, she sauntered towards the kitchen. "Go make yourself comfortable at the table, I'm going to get the steak from the oven," She winked at Kayla, "I was keeping it warm while I waited for you."

Kayla took in the well-dressed table with golden, tapered candles at either end. A beautiful centerpiece of roses and fallen petals floated in a fish bowl-like vase. The bone china dishes gleamed on golden charger plates. Her heart swelled with pleasure at the sight and the trouble that Liz took in creating this special evening.

Liz returned a moment later pushing a serving cart carrying a platter with two, thick-cut porterhouse steaks, sizzling in *au jus*, a bowl with mashed sweet potatoes and another with roasted asparagus.

"Hmmm," Kayla said sensuously. The sound vibrated and hung in the air.

Liz's tongue flicked between her lips as she darted a quick glance at Kayla through her lashes. With deliberate movements, she served Kayla and herself then she reached for the bottle of *Cabernet Sauvignon.*

"I'll do the honors," Kayla whispered, her fingers lightly grazed the inside of Liz' wrist as she took the bottle and opened it. She filled both their wine glasses and sat to eat.

"I hope you like your steak medium-rare" Liz said as Kayla reached for her steak knife.

"Lucky for you I do," Kayla laughed.

"It's so nice to finally have some alone time with you after everything... Kayla continued, smiling at Liz.

"That's why you should take up my offer and move in with us, that way we can have all the alone time we need when you get home from work."

"I should....," Kayla agreed jokingly, "I think I can get used to a candlelit dinner every evening." They both laughed.

"So how was your day...?" Liz asked, leaning towards Kayla.

"Did anything interesting happen at work today? She peered deep into Kayla's eyes, willing her to mention the flowers.

"My day was mostly meetings," Kayla responded. I didn't get to my office until minutes to two in the afternoon. You know how it is with these wealthy clients, they are very particular and high maintenance when it comes to their wealth."

Liz leaned forward in her chair toward Kayla, her eyes veiled. "Yeah I understand." After a distinct pause where they ate companionably, Liz tried again. "Anything else out of the ordinary? She asked, examining her steak with much fascination.

"I don't believe so," Kayla said as she reached for her glass of wine. She took a sip. "It was pretty ordinary for the most part …" The memory of those confounded flowers careened through her mind. Why would James send her flowers? He was up to his old tricks. Should she mention this incident to Liz? She did not want lies or hidden truths to be a part of their fledgling relationship. With a furrowed brow she blurted out: "Except for one thing …"

Liz looked at her in feigned surprise. "Oh?"

"Well, when I got back to the office in the afternoon, there was a vase of Stargazer Lilies waiting for me on my desk. You won't believe who sent them."

"An admirer?" Liz responded, trying to sound clueless.

"No, they were sent by James, or at least that's what the note said…"

"Oh really," Liz replied, stuffing her mouth with salad, trying to hide the obvious surprise on her face; surprised that Kayla was honest with her. She expected that Kayla would keep any contact with James from her. "What did the note say?" she asked.

"It just said, *I miss you. . .Love James*' Kayla said. "I still can't figure out why he would send me flowers and how he knows where I work..., did you say anything to him?" She asked with much curiosity.

"No, I didn't. I saw him earlier today when I stopped by to get David's rocking pony, but we didn't talk much, except for updating him on our meeting next Monday, to discuss the schedule for us sharing the kids. You'll learn quickly that James has his ways when it comes to the opposite sex. He's like a wolf who can sniff out his prey from a mile away," Liz said, trying to fill Kayla's mind with past thoughts of James.

"I haven't given it much thought since then," Kayla responded. "I asked my assistant to discard them and that was it. ...."

Liz raised her glass in the air. "Let's not spend this evening talking about James, How about dessert?"

"Sure," Kayla said as she poured more wine in her glass.

Liz sliced and served the *Pavlova*. "This is really good," Kayla said as she savored the first bite.

"I'm glad you like it, it's about the only dessert I can't mess up." Liz joked,

Kayla chuckled at the expression on Liz' face. "It's also my favorite dessert."

"Really?" Liz joined in the laughter. "What a coincidence, it's my favorite dessert too, and the fresh strawberries are like the icing on top. It's so funny how we have more in common than we realize: Our knack for sophistication, we are at our happiest when we are the bosses of our own lives, we have the same taste in food and wine, and as much as I hate to say it we even have the same taste in men...." Kayla looked at Liz and they both giggled.

Later that evening, after eating the entire *Pavlova* and finishing their third bottle of wine, Kayla offered to do the dishes since Liz made dinner. They made small talk and jokes as they cleaned the dishes; Kayla washing and Liz drying. When Liz dried the last wine glass, she went up behind Kayla who was still standing at the sink drying her hands. She ran her fingers through Kayla's hair, gently side-sweeping the thick locks and slowly kissing her along her ear down to her neck. Kayla took a deep breath as Liz's warm breath touched her neck, she slowly closed her eyes and grasped the sink.

"I have missed you," Liz whispered in her ear.

Kayla turned around to face Liz. They kissed each other fervently, deep intense and satisfying. In every breath they took, soft passionate moans escaped from their mouths. There was no denying that they both wanted each other.

Liz took Kayla's hands and led her up the stairs to her bedroom. She gently pushed Kayla down on the bed and straddled her. After a while, she flipped Kayla onto her belly, and slowly unzipped Kayla's dress. She proceeded to trace Kayla's spine from the nape of her neck to just where her curves met her perfectly statuesque bottom. Groping Kayla's bottom, Liz' teeth nibbled and played with the band of Kayla's thong. With eyes closed, Kayla moaned softly, she could feel every hair on her body awaken as Liz pushed her boundaries increasing her libido.

She turned over onto her back and sat up to undress Liz. She gently sucked on Liz's perky pink nipples while her right hand traced its way to her already wet cleft. Liz grabbed onto Kayla's right hand, guiding it deeper between her thighs, her moans increased as she moved Kayla's hand back and forth sending shivering sensation through her clitoris and labia.

Kayla laid Liz down on the bed and slid her fingers inside Liz's dripping slit. The louder Liz moaned the more Kayla increased the thrusting of her fingers, deeper and deeper reaching her cervix. Liz's hands scrunched the bed sheets as she got closer to climax, her legs shivered and her waist danced, her breathing escalated and her knees buckled. With a shuddering gasp she climaxed, shaking under Kayla's body. Kayla kissed her and ran her finger through her thick fiery red hair. Both panting...; their bodies tried to recover from the extraordinary pleasure.

"Have I told you lately that I love you?" Liz whispered to Kayla, staring deep into her eyes. Her chest was still moving up and down and her voice sounding as if she could barely breathe. "Kayla leaned in and kissed her and rolled over to lay beside her. She kissed her again on the cheek and rose from the bed to walk to the bathroom. Liz followed shortly behind her. Liz slid the glass door of the shower open and went in behind her. Kayla turned to face her and they both kissed and caressed each other's wet skin, as the warm water flowed down their bodies.

Liz knelt down and raised Kayla's left leg over her shoulder, she used her tongue to gently tease Kayla's throbbing clitoris. Her tongue worked its way from Kayla's clitoris to the entrance of her vestibule. She used her tongue to stoke Kayla's clitoris, making her wetter and wetter on each stroke. Kayla braced her back on the glass shower door while her hips swayed uncontrollably from the pleasurable torment of Liz's tongue. Kayla screamed in ecstasy as she grabbed Liz's hair.

Liz moved her tongue back to Kayla's clitoris as she used her fingers to continue the strokes. Kayla could no longer control the movement of her body. The leg she stood on lost all feeling as the blood ran to her clit and labia. Her grip of Liz's hair tightened and her eyes rolled back as she exploded in another climax. Her body quivered from intense pleasure. Liz stood up and they shared an intense kiss, giving Kayla the opportunity to taste herself. They washed each other's body, both mesmerized by how great the sex was. In Kayla's mind she was falling deeper for Liz, and in Liz's mind things were working out as planned and she was now convinced she could take the next step.

They retired to bed shortly after, both too tired to do anything else but kiss good night. As Kayla slowly fell asleep, she imagined what life with Liz would be like and the thought made her smile. She was happy and in a much better head space through all that had happened and she was confident that her relationship with Liz would only get better.

At 5:30 am Kayla was awakened by her insistent alarm. Beside her, Liz cuddled her pillow in deep sleep. Even in sleep, void of makeup, Liz was still beautiful. Warmth flooded Kayla as she thought of the peaks they reached together last night. On impulse, she reached over and pressed her lips to Liz' forehead. Oh, how she loved this woman!

Kayla made her way to the bathroom. Turning on the faucet, she cupped both hands to splash water on her face then froze in shock. As the water coursed through her fingers, she stared in disbelief at her finger adorned with a huge diamond ring! Her heart skipped a beat as a million and one thoughts raced through her head, one of which was that this ring must have cost a fortune.

She turned around to run back to the bedroom but met Liz who was standing at the bathroom door. Kayla stopped in her tracks and looked at Liz, then down at the ring, shaking her head as tears ran down her cheeks.

"Will you marry me?" Liz asked, walking towards her. "I know it may seem like I'm moving too fast, but what do we really need to wait for?

Kayla looked dumbstruck, her lips moved but there was no sound.

Liz raised her outstretched arms as she slowly walked towards Kayla. "What else do we need to convince us that we are meant for each other? I know I love you, and I believe that you love me too...so can we make us official?"

Kayla nodded her head and ran into Liz's arms, choked up from all the emotions she was feeling. She had no reason to not accept Liz's proposal, after all, that's all she had ever wanted, to find someone she loved and who loved her back, great sex, stability and marriage, she finally had all that and so much more.

"Kayla...," Liz said looking into her eyes, "I want to hear you say it. Will you marry me...will you be mine for the rest of our lives?"

Kayla looked at her and gazed at the ring sparkling back at her. With heart pounding, hands shaking, and tears trickling down her face, she looked Liz in the eyes, kissed her and whispered, "Yes I will...I will marry you...."

Chapter 10

James returned from his 5 am run and turned on his computer to find an email from his old friend, Asher, about a job offer. He quickly dialed the number. "Hey Asher, it James...how are you? It's great to hear from you. I'm calling in regard to your email... so you may have something for me?"

"Hey James, yeah, my firm has something coming up that you may be interested in. How about lunch today and I'll give you some more details?"

"Yeah," James replied, "I can do lunch, where do I meet you?"

"At Café Délice, say around...1:00 p.m?

"Sure, I'll be there...see you then." James smiled as he hung up the phone. They have been great friends for a long time. Asher would only suggest a job if he was sure to get it.

James began a soft whistle as he tossed his sweaty shirt in the hamper. He felt confident that he would have a job by his next meeting with Elizabeth.

Kayla entered her office at around 8 am, as if she were walking on clouds; still enraptured by the previous night's events. She was engaged to be married! She opened the blinds of her office window and just observed the scenery. From time-to-time she glanced down at the big rock on her finger, winking back at her. A satisfied smile tugged at the corners of her mouth.

Lisa knocked on her door before walking in. "Good morning Miss Riviera," she said as she walked over to Kayla's desk. "Should we go over this morning's agenda?"

"Hey Lisa," Kayla said, stepping towards her desk and pulling out her chair. As she sat, she fisted her left hand into her right to casually cover her diamond ring. She wanted to hug the news to herself for a bit longer before she shared it with the outside world. "Sure, what is my day like today?"

"Well, you have a 9:30 am with Myers & Myers' CFO; it's more of a formality meeting where you will discuss the investment and allocation options for their portfolio."

"Oh yeah, I remember that ..." Kayla responded, scrolling through her tablet. "I prepared a briefing for them yesterday morning, I did some research on them so I have a handle on what they are looking for. I happened to have managed a subsidiary account of theirs, back in Vancouver, so I'm familiar with their portfolio... what else?"

"The CEO flew in yesterday," Lisa continued. "He wants a lunch meeting with you to discuss some strategies for the upcoming 'meeting of minds events' slated for the end of this month."

"That meeting is today?" Kayla asked with a dazed look on her face. "I could have sworn I had that meeting down for Friday?"

"It was originally scheduled for Friday. However, he flew in early and decided to move up the meeting date, I literally added it to your calendar this morning...I know its short notice but he didn't give me much of a choice. What do they really do at a 'meeting of minds event'? Lisa asked, with a curious expression on her face; "I've never been able to attend one of those events, always seem so top secret."

Kayla gazed at her with a smile...more so because she was a bit astounded that there was something that Lisa didn't know much about. "It's not as top secret as it seems," Kayla responded. "It's really a platform that serves three diverse financial services communities; Private Banking and Wealth Management companies like us, Financial Advisory and I believe Bank and Brand Distribution. The only reason you were never able to attend one of those events is because the invited audience are usually those at CEO and CIO levels and senior decision-makers like myself, responsible for overseeing the company's financial services strategies. It's really an elaborate meeting for networking at the highest level. It also comes with the perks of gaining exclusive access to community research and ways for companies like ours to gather strategic insight and explore business development opportunities, trust me... you don't really want to go."

"I see..." Lisa said, flicking the pen in her hand. "That's why this time of the year the office is crawling with rich, old geezers, walking about with their noses in the air." She chuckled. "You're right, I don't think I'd enjoy being in a room with those people...." She continued to scroll through her tablet, picking up where she left off with Kayla's calendar. Kayla shook her head and smiled at Lisa's comment.

"And finally," Lisa continued. "The bulk of your day will be spent analyzing the financial information we obtained from our two new potential clients: Tech billionaire, Jude Dawes and multi-millionaire, Aiden Kyles, to regulate strategies to meet their financial objectives. We have to get back to them early next week so it is imperative we get a head start on the financial planning and recommendations." Lisa looked over to Kayla for instructions holding her tablet to the side.

"I'm ready for everything except the meeting with the CEO." Kayla said looking up at Lisa. "I'll have to put something together before lunch, so I'm going to need your help with a few documents if I'm going to get it done on time." Kayla signaled to Lisa to come over to her side of the desk. As Kayla pointed to her computer screen, briefing Lisa on some pointers for the strategies, Lisa's eyes widened as she caught sight of the diamond on Kayla's finger.

"Oh my God!" she squealed in surprise and excitement. "Look at the size of that thing." Kayla turned to look at her, a bit confused at the sudden outburst, Lisa's eyes still focused on her finger made her instantly aware of what Lisa's outburst was about.

"You're engaged?" Lisa asked, reaching out to hold Kayla's finger. "I didn't even know you were dating, not that it is my place to know those things but I mean...wow!"

Kayla smiled at her diffidently. "It happened last night," she responded, pulling her finger from Lisa's grip. "And you are right, it's not your place to know these things; but I understand and share your excitement, so thank you. Now can we get back to work?"

Despite Kayla's unwillingness to share details of the engagement with Lisa, the expression on Lisa's face showed that she was just dying to know who, what, when. She reluctantly turned her attention back to Kayla's computer, and every now and then helplessly stared on the ring.

Kayla briefed Lisa on the documents she wanted done and Lisa left her office shortly after. She looked at her watch and saw that it was close to her 9:30 consultation with Myers and Myers. She grabbed her tablet and bag and left the office.

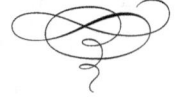

Chapter 11

At about a 12:45 pm James walked into Café Délice and took a seat by the window. A waitress walked over to him and gave him a menu after pleasantries and going through the specials. As he went through the menu, he caught sight of Asher coming towards the Café from the opposite parking lot. As he entered, James signaled him over to their table.

"James, it's been what...two-three months?"

"About that...," James replied locking hands with Asher to do their familiar greet. "Things have been busy in the last three months, James continued, signaling the waitress over. "Divorce, custody battle, all my ties and connection expunged from the firm...you name it, I've been through it; the last three months have been a whirlwind."

"So, it's true?" Asher asked. "I won't lie, I have heard the chatter and I have seen your face splashed on a few gossip columns but you know you can't always believe the gossip. You know me, I prefer to hear it from the horse's mouth." They both took some time to place their orders with the waitress before continuing the conversation.

"Why the hell would Elizabeth kick you out of the firm, is a divorce not enough these days, they have to take everything."

"It's a long story Asher, the short of the matter is the Elizabeth I married has changed. She's now crazy, controlling, and manipulative. She's vindictive and treacherous..."

"Wait...Wait..."Asher interjected. "What do you mean she has changed? She sounds exactly like the Elizabeth I knew back in law school."

"What do you mean?" James asked, sounding confused.

"Crazy, controlling, manipulative, vindictive and treacherous; that's Elizabeth in a nutshell," Asher said with a grin.

"What are you talking about?" James asked, still sounding confused.

"James," Asher said in a patient voice, "Elizabeth was always like you described, you were just too in love to see it. You don't believe me? Ok... do you remember Ava Murano?" James knitted his brow trying to remember.

"Ava Murano..." Asher continued. "Tall, blonde, blue eyed wildcat that was head over heels in love with you back in law school. She tried tirelessly to get your attention months before you started hanging out with Elizabeth. You remember that bonfire party we had in our second year?"

"Yeah I remember the party," James answered.

"She intentionally spilled her drinks on your pants so she could grab your crotch," Asher's voice cracked in hilarity.

"Oh her," James said as he recalled who she was. "What about her?" he asked Asher, trying to figure out how she related to Asher's perception of Elizabeth.

Asher's eyes lit up as he got more eager to prove his point to James. "You took Elizabeth to that party, but Ava was still after you, she walked up to you pretending to be drunk and spilled her drink on your pants. You didn't realize it...but while she was there groping your crotch in the name of drying the liquid, Elizabeth was fuming, the way she looked at Ava it was like she would kill her if she could."

"When you went to the restroom to clean up, Elizabeth grabbed Ava and took her aside on the beach. I never heard what she said to her that night but Ava left the beach and her interest in you dwindled after that. About two months after that party, Ava lost her sponsorship and got kicked out of law school from an anonymous tip to her sponsors that she was misusing her funding and abusing hard drugs."

"Are you saying Elizabeth had her kicked out of law school?" James asked sounding unconvinced. "She was abusing hard drugs, that's one of the reasons I never gave her the light of day. Are you sure it wasn't just coincidence that her sponsors found out?"

"Look man," Asher said trying to convince James. "I never thought much of it then either, until I ran into Ava a year ago. We got to talking and she happened to ask about you. I told her you were now married to Elizabeth and heading her family firm. The look on her face at the mention of Elizabeth's name was as if she was experiencing the holocaust. She was terrified. She said when Elizabeth drew her aside that night, she told her that when she got what was coming to her she should remember that she messed with the wrong woman's man. She said Elizabeth told her things about her and her family that she never told anyone in law school."

James gaped at Asher, his jaw slack. "You're kidding me, right?"

"Elizabeth told her that she would never graduate from law school let alone practice law in California as long as she had anything to do with it. Months later she was kicked out and lost her sponsorship." It turned out that Elizabeth's father was chairman on the board of the institution that sponsored Ava. Do you still think that was a coincidence"?

"Ava said Elizabeth was there the day she was dismissed, waiting outside for her with a parting gloat, reminding her that she messed with the wrong woman's man."

"We both know that Ava had a wild side but she would have been a damn good lawyer because she never flunked any of the exams we took, and she always aced the practice cases. Her sponsorship was her only way to get through law school and Elizabeth ripped it right out from under her because she flirted with you."

"James, Elizabeth has been treacherous from the get go, and controlling...don't get me started, once you started dating her you never went anywhere unless she said you could or unless she could tag along. But, you were so blinded by love you couldn't see what we saw. If you once forgot her birthday or your so-called relationship anniversary she would have a fit. She wouldn't speak to you for days, and you would have to shower her with gifts and public displays of how sorry you were before she would forgive you. Face it James, she practically had you by the balls. man... that girl is crazy."

James sat there stunned as he finally started to see the validity in what Asher was saying. Elizabeth didn't change as he had thought. The scales of love that had blinded his eyes then to Elizabeth' true form had started to peel away the moment her ways started to get overbearing. The scales of love disappeared completely the instant he fell out of love with her, and that's when he had really started to see who she was all along.

He retreated into his thoughts trying to come to terms with how blind he really was. Asher calling his name snapped him out of his reverie.

"You are lucky she didn't use her connections to blacklist you from practicing law in California like she did to Ava..." Asher said taking a bite of his sandwich. "She must still really love you or she's just not done with you yet."

"Kayla" James said under his breath, with an expression on his face as if he had just had an epiphany. "Kayla is her knight."

"Who is Kayla?" Asher asked, thrown off by James sudden interjection of another name into the conversation. "And when did our conversation time travel to medieval times...why is she a knight?"

"That's not what I mean," James said, trying to gather his thoughts to explain to Asher. "Elizabeth often uses the chess pieces as an analogy to describe the people in her lives. She did that all through our marriage, most of it sarcastically or so I thought, she told me yesterday that I was a pawn in her game of chess, practically telling me that I was the weakest piece."

"She also said Kayla had proven her love and allegiance to her and was no longer a pawn but could be a queen. But now that I think about it she was just trying to throw me off, she won't make Kayla the queen because Kayla is her knight, my destruction."

Asher looked at him trying to wrap his head around what James was babbling about. "Again, I ask, who is Kayla?"

"Kayla is the girl I met when I went to Vancouver a couple of years ago, she's the one I had my first affair with that transitioned into a full-blown relationship that lasted for almost eight years. She's the girl I told you I fell in love with—that if it were not for my kids I would have divorced Elizabeth in a heartbeat to be with her."

"Oh...that is Kayla," Asher responded as he recalled James' story. "I don't think you ever told me her name...but how is she Elizabeth's 'Knight' as you put it. What does she have to do with anything? As far as you told me, it was a secret affair and when Elizabeth found out you broke it off, so how is she now involved?"

James shook his head and made an exasperating laugh as it was all suddenly making sense in his head. "She is here in California..." he said to Asher. Asher's eyes bulged in disbelief "And that's not the craziest part..." James continued. "She's shacking up with Elizabeth." Asher almost choked on a sip of his drink.

"She's what?" He exclaimed. "How the fuck did that happen; how they even met?"

"That's what I've been trying to wrap my head around from the very day I found out," James replied. "Kayla told me in not so many words that they met by coincidence and she didn't know who Elizabeth was until later in their relationship when Elizabeth used her to catch me cheating."

"My God, this sounds so...so ..."

"Diabolical? Right. When I confronted Elizabeth about my suspicions of her relationship with Kayla yesterday, she denied my allegations, saying she met Kayla by coincidence at *WhisPer*. But later in the conversation I started to realize that she had a hand in Kayla's move to California, I don't know how but I'm convinced she does."

"Wait…Wait…Wait"… Asher said in a curious tone, trying to absorb it all, "You mean you have spoken to Kayla, and she knows Elizabeth is your wife, well ex-wife, and she's ok with that? What the fuck is going on in your life? This is like a real live soap opera. Why the fuck would Elizabeth want to shack up with your one-time mistress…what…I…a…"

"You don't get it do you?" James cut him off. "Elizabeth is not just shacking up with Kayla because of some mere coincidence. This is a game for Elizabeth, this is a way for her to use Kayla against me…just another game of chess for Elizabeth and in this game, she has made Kayla her Knight."

"You play chess so you understand what I'm saying right? James asked Asher eager for him to understand. "The Knight is one of the most dangerous and powerful pieces in the game. If a Knight is used strategically, his abilities can by far outweigh what the queen can do. Don't you see? Knights are valuable in the middle of the board; so, for Elizabeth, Kayla is much more valuable to her if she is placed in the middle of our controversy. We have a saying in chess 'A knight on the rim is dim'; if Elizabeth had let Kayla remained in Vancouver, she would be of no use to her, because chances are, after the divorce, I would have gone right back to Vancouver looking for her, and Elizabeth knows this, she now knows Kayla holds my heart."

Asher shook his head from side to side, looking askance at James as if he had suddenly sprouted two horns.

James sighed and rubbed his two hands together. "If Elizabeth gets Kayla in her corner and succeeds in completely turning her mind against me, and we both know that Elizabeth is very manipulative, there's no telling what she can get Kayla to do to me. Or even worse, what she could do to Kayla just to hurt me. This is not good…" James continued; looking as if he was about to panic.

"Calm down," Asher said, trying to deflate James worry. "Why don't you just talk to Kayla, get her to understand what Elizabeth is really after?"

"It's not that simple," James responded. "She made it clear when she confronted me that her new-found relationship with Elizabeth and my kids would give her the ammunition she needed to make my life a living hell."

Asher pursed his lips and let out a whooshing sound. "Man, you are strung up by the balls."

"That's for sure. And … If you recall, I wasn't really honest with Kayla when I met her. I practically hid the fact that I was married and had children. When Elizabeth found out and gave me that ultimatum I had no choice but to break it off, for the sake of my kids and for Kayla's safety. If Elizabeth fuels that fire like I think she will, then there's no telling what hell is about to break loose in my life."

"Man, this is crazy" Asher interjected with a stunned expression on his face. "You practically have two scorned women plotting against you. One crazy as hell and out to destroy you because you refused to be her puppet, and the other out for revenge for breaking her heart...man you are truly screwed. In all seriousness..., it seems like you are really in love with this Kayla girl, if that is the case you have to find a way to make her understand what really transpired back then, and what Elizabeth is trying to do now. We both know that Elizabeth is unpredictable, so it's best to act fast before she perfects whatever it is she is concocting."

James ran his fingers through his hair. "I know, I know."

"I have to go back to the office soon, so regarding the job, my firm has just taken on the case of a major Pharmaceutical company here in California that is being sued for product liability. The paperwork alone for this case is going to require an army to divide and conquer if we are going to have a chance at winning for our client. This is a civil litigation matter and you are one of the best litigators I know. It's still your passion right...?"

"Yes, it still is," James responded eagerly.

"Then that settles it," Asher responded. "I've already explained to my boss why he needs to hire you on this case, so it's just a matter of coming into the office on Monday when he returns from a short trip he took on another case. We can go over the formalities of hiring you to work on the case then."

"Monday..." James responded hesitantly.

"What... is something wrong with Monday?'

"I'm supposed to be meeting with Elizabeth on Monday to finalize the custody schedule, to decide on the dates that I get to be with the kids... it won't be a problem..." James continued, as he tried to reassure Asher. "Just let me know the time of the meeting on Monday and I'll make sure to meet with Elizabeth before or after.

"I can let you know by Friday," Asher agreed. "Do keep me in the loop," he said referring to James predicament as he got up from the table. "Take care man…" they locked hands again and Asher left.

James left the café shortly after. On the drive home, he tried to figure out a way to get in touch with Kayla. He couldn't just walk up to Elizabeth's home and ask for her, that would be suicide. Without knowing exactly where she worked, finding her otherwise seemed near impossible.

Besides, even if he did find where she worked, she wouldn't just welcome him with open arms and ears to listen to what he had to say. As far as she was concerned, James was a liar and a cheat. Who knows what other things Elizabeth had said to poison Kayla's mind against him? The task seemed worse the more he thought about it.

He knew he couldn't live with himself if something happened to Kayla because of him. He had to tell her the real reason why he left her back in Vancouver and the real reason why he hid his other life away from her, she deserved to know. But how?

Chapter 12

When James got home he was so unsettled that he paced around the living room for several minutes just trying to figure out where to start. How to reach out to Kayla without alerting Elizabeth? It suddenly hit him. He knew where she worked back in Vancouver, at least he knew what kind of job she did. What if he made a call to her previous company in Vancouver, pretended to be an old client looking for her; maybe then he could possibly get her contact details here in California.

He immediately got his phone and searched for Wealth Management Companies in the Vancouver area where he knew Kayla worked. He was lucky, his search gave him six possible companies and so he recorded their numbers and started to call. The first three numbers he called were no good, they have never employed a Kayla Riviera. He was on the line to the fifth company on his list when the person on the line told him to hold for transfer.

"Matthew Perez speaking, how may I be of help?" When Kayla was promoted to the California office, Matthew had instructed the company receptionist Elyssa, to direct incoming calls for Kayla to his desk, so naturally, when James called the company asking for Kayla Riviera, Elyssa transferred him to her former boss Matthew Perez.

At the sound of Matthew's voice, James hesitated to gather his thoughts on what he was about to say. "Hello... this is James Cassidy, I'm trying to reach Kayla Riviera, I met her when I was on business in Vancouver some years ago and she gave me her card that I could call her should I need her wealth management services. I am looking to fly in to Vancouver this weekend and was hoping I could make an appointment to have a consultation with her."

"Hello James," Matthew replied, "I am Kayla's former boss, she is no longer at the Vancouver office, but I would be happy to meet with you for a consultation when you fly in." James hesitated, "really, where is she now?" he asked Matthew.

"She's has been promoted to our California office, she still consults with us so you'd be happy to know that should you become a client she'd also be involved in the assessment and investment decision making process of your portfolio."

"Did you say she's in California?" James asked, *phishing* for more information. What a coincidence, I live in California, but I didn't know she was here. That's even better, if you give me her contact information here, I'll be sure to reach out to her."

"Sure," Matthew responded, "Do you have a pen?"

James quickly looked around the room and grabbed a pen that was laying on the coffee table and flipped a magazine close by to a blank spot where he could record the information.

"I've got one..." James responded.

"Ok," Matthew continued. "The phone number for the California office is 464-0041, you may also contact her via email at kayla.riviera@DMCWealth.ca

"Got it," James said, trying to quell his elation. "Thanks for the information, I appreciate it."

"You are most welcome, Mr. Cassidy, do take care now." Matthew hung up.

James finally had what he needed to reach out to Kayla, he didn't want to email her, as he knew she'd probably ignore his emails. He didn't want to try and get her over the phone either as he knew she'd probably hang up the moment she realized it was him. He had to get a meeting with her. "That's it!" he exclaimed, "Call her office, make an appointment under a fake name, that way she won't know it's me until I'm right there in front of her."

And that's exactly what he did or at least tried to do. James called DMC Wealth Management with the hopes of making an appointment to meet with Kayla, but during the first few sentences of the conversation with Victor, the receptionist, James realized that a meeting with Kayla was not going to be as easy as he had thought.

"So, Mr. Chase" (the fake name James was using); Victor said. "To schedule a consultation with Miss Riviera you first need to complete the application form I'll be sending to your email, and then forward same to Mrs. Riviera's email. She'll assess your profile information based on our Wealth Management client criteria and if your profile meets the requirement she will contact you. After that you can both decide on the dates and place to meet."

In keeping up the pretense there wasn't much James could say but to provide Victor with an email address where he could forward the form before he hung up. He scanned through the form that got to his email minutes later and realized he was back to square one with his plans. There was no way he could honestly complete this form with a fake identity. The form required, passport and driver's licenses number, bank information, and source(s) of wealth. He had none of that information for fake name, John Chase. His only option would be to put his own information which made no sense because he knew Kayla would just reject it anyway. He was back to square one...

James sat on the coach by the coffee table and did some thinking for a minute, trying to recall if there was anyone he knew with connections to the company. Who could possibly help him to get a sit down with Kayla without going through the regular process? He thought long and hard but came up with nothing. He was halfway up the stairs to change into something more casual when it hit him. He suddenly remembered he had a friend whose father dabbled in Wealth Management. It was a long shot because he didn't know if Brad's father would have any connection specific to Kayla's company at all, but hell, it was worth a try.

He quickly scrolled through his phone to find Brad's number and called him.

"Hey Brad, what's up man, it James..."

"Yeah James what's going on?" replied Brad.

"Look man, this may sound a little unorthodox but I'm hoping you can help," said James.

"Ok..." Brad replied hesitantly. What is it...?"

"If I'm not mistaking, your dad has some connections in a major wealth management company here, right?"

"Yeah he does…where are you going with this?" Brad replied, sounding a bit confused as to what exactly James wanted him to do.

"I'm getting to that," James replied anxiously. "By any Chance is the Wealth Management Company DMC Wealth?"

"Actually, it is," Brad replied. "Look James are you going to skip the twenty questions and get straight into why you called me? I was actually on my way out when you called."

"I promise I won't take much more of your time, just hear me out" James replied rambling. "I need to get a meeting with the new appointed Wealth Manager Kayla Riviera, it's a matter of life and death that I speak to her as soon as possible but she cannot know that I'm the one she would be meeting with. Can you get your dad to make this happen?" He practically held his breath waiting for Brad's response.

"Wait…" Brad said trying to make sense of James request. "Why don't you want this person to know who you are…what kind of trouble are you in James?"

"I'm not in any trouble," James snapped. "It's a long story and like you said you don't have the time, I promise I'll tell you all about it if you can make it happen."

"Ok…ok, don't get your boxers in a bunch," Brad joked at James's obvious irritation at his question. "I think I can be of help, my dad served on DMC's advisory board of directors for some years now, but he stepped down last month" James was about to interrupt when Brad stopped him.

"…Wait I'm not finished…" Brad continued, "I said I could be of help right…so just let me finish. My dad stepped down last month, however I took his place. I think I know who you are talking about too, I met her in a board meeting a day ago. I tell you one thing, she is fine as hell, and I think I know why you want to meet with her anonymously, because I know it has nothing to do with managing your wealth." Brad said in a perverse tone. "But let me ask you one question," Brad continued. "Why don't you get your wife to set up the meeting if it's a matter of 'life and death' as you put it, she also sits on the board of directors, she has more voting rights than I do, so naturally she'd be able to pull more strings than I can."

"James was dumb struck. He had no clue Elizabeth was on the board of directors at Kayla's company. "What else has she been hiding?" He mumbled under his breath.

Brad was still waiting for an answer. "So why don't you ask your wife?" he continued.

"I can't," James answered. "We are divorced, and we didn't end things on the best of terms so she won't be in a hurry to help me with anything."

"You said you were in a board meeting with Kayla a day ago right? Was Elizabeth there? James asked, trying to figure out if Kayla knew.

"No, she wasn't there," Brad replied. "She's one of those advisory members that prefer to be kept anonymous. They make their suggestions/directions known only to the CEO and the top executives who then carries out their bidding for lack of a better word. I only know your wife is on the board because my dad knew her dad and knows that she's the one that took over when he died. You know they are crazy rich right…and with her money she has a great deal of power and influence. You were married to her so you must know. Her dad advised on the board of directors for some of the largest companies across California. And since his passing, she has replaced her dad in all those ventures. How can you not know that?"

"Who said I didn't know?" James replied in a defensive tone. "My knowledge of my wife's affluence has nothing to do with what I'm asking you. Besides, as I said, we are divorced now so none of that matters…so will you help me?"

Brad made a snickering laugh at James obvious ignorance towards the information about his wife before he answered his question. "Yeah, as I said I may be able to help, I believe Kayla's personal assistant Lisa, has a little crush on me, I'll call her up, see what she can do."

"Thanks man, I owe you one," James said with a sigh of relief. "And remember, she can't know that she's meeting with me. Tell her it's one of your colleagues or something. Use a fake name if you have to…and see if her assistant can schedule the meeting outside of her office, like a Café or restaurant…you know what… make it Café Délice sometime before the end of this week, I'll work with whatever time she's available."

"I'll do my best boss," Brad replied sarcastically. "I'll let you know what Lisa says when I call her. I have to go now. Talk later." Brad hung up.

James changed out of formal attire into a t-shirt and sweat pants and went to the kitchen to get something to eat. The entire time he imagined meeting with Kayla and replaying scenarios in his head of what he hoped their meeting would be. He practically spent the rest of the day on pins and needles, watching his phone, praying for Brad to call with good news.

At about 5:45 p.m, Brad called. "You are lucky Lisa really likes me, you are in. I told her you are a very wealthy, important colleague of mine looking for a reputable Wealth Manager to have a brief consultation regarding the management of your wealth. Lisa assured me she would fit you into Kayla's schedule for 2:30 pm tomorrow at your selected location Café Délice. You only have half an hour because she as another meeting at 3 pm, so make it count.....you owe me big time."

"I do... I owe you big time." James agreed. "Thanks man, you are a great friend, I'll remember this next time your wife calls looking for you. I won't hesitate to lie on your behalf," James joked.

"Funny," Brad said laughing sarcastically. "I can handle my wife, can't say I can say the same about you," he jabbed. "Anyway man, go do your thing...take care and we'll talk soon."

"Yeah we'll talk soon," James replied as he hung up the phone. Anticipation and anxiety coursed through his body. He couldn't wait for tomorrow. At last he was going to have his say with Kayla.

Chapter 13

On Thursday morning Kayla, walked into the office, practically floating on clouds after another amazing night with Liz. She was convinced now more than ever that she had finally found love with Liz. The sex was amazing, she didn't hover, she had class and sophistication, affluence and wealth. And the constant reminder of how much Liz loved her was symbolized by the enormous, shiny diamond on her finger. If she had any doubt about marrying Liz, it all went away after last night.

At her desk, she browsed through her emails and to-do-list to get a picture of what her day was going to look like. Physically, her body was in the office but her mind was still stuck at home with Liz. The ear-to-ear smile and pinked cheeks gave her thoughts away when Lisa walked in.

"I can see that you are very happy," Lisa said with a smile. "Have you decided on a date yet, and when am I going to meet him …?"

Kayla stopped her before she could ask any more questions. "Good morning to you too Lisa" she said with a hint of sarcasm.

"I thought I made it clear before, I don't discuss my personal life at the office. It's better for everyone if the two are kept separate. I appreciate you being happy for me, however, unless you find out on your own you won't be hearing anything from me.

As Lisa shook her head in consternation, Kayla thought she may have been a little harsh. So., she plastered on a professional smile to soften the impact of her words. She quickly changed the subject and said in a cheery voice, "What do you have for me this morning...did you complete the last-minute brief I requested before I came in this morning."

"Yes, I did," Lisa answered promptly, as she walked over to Kayla's desk to hand her the folder with the brief. "Here you go..." she murmured, a little embarrassed and not quite meeting Kayla's eyes.

Kayla smiled at her as she took the folder and quickly flipped through it. "It seems to be in order..." she said softly as she looked over the last page. "Is there anything else I need to be prepared for today, any surprise visits or presentations?"

"No surprise visits or presentations..."Lisa replied as she scrolled through a copy of Kayla's calendar on her tablet, you do however have a last-minute consultation that I added to your schedule late yesterday".

"It's a favor called in from a member of our board of di-rectors..." Lisa continued "...It should be a brief meeting no more than half an hour. You will be meeting with a potential wealthy client who needs an expert's breakdown of the wealth management process; which he believes will help him better make a decision if wealth management is right for him..."

"So why couldn't one of the wealth advisors meet with him…." Kayla asked with an expression on her face that told Lisa she needed to justify why she had to be the one to meet with this potential client.

Lisa knew the true reason why she added the request to Kayla's calendar, but seeing that Kayla had no interest in personal agendas she couldn't dare tell her the truth….

"Apparently the client is a colleague of one of our prominent member on the board of directors and they recommended that you meet with the client being that he has the potential to be a high-profile client."

"Well, I guess I don't have a choice," Kayla mumbled under her breath. "So, what else should I know about this client, does he have a name…what does he look like?"

Lisa flipped through the papers on her lap. "According to the information I received his name is Duke Duero…and he prefers to meet at Café Délice; he knows who you are so he will be waiting for you. I penciled him in for 2:00 p.m which was the only opening on your schedule today…I hope that is ok?"

"That's fine Lisa," Kayla replied, looking up at Lisa again with a less than happy smile. "If that is all, please feel free to leave, I have a Skype call with the 'The Dragon' before I meet with the new prospect."

"Oh…" Lisa mouthed softly. "Yikes…ok then good luck, don't let me keep you," she said as she exited Kayla's office. She really felt bad that Kayla was starting her morning with a Skype call to 'The Dragon' but was happy she wasn't in Kayla's shoes. 'The Dragon' was a nickname they both gave to Kayla's client who was most difficult to deal with. They were convinced that there was nothing on earth that could please this man. He was always fuming, always agitated and always skeptical of Kayla's wealth management tactics and investment recommendations. He was an older gentleman, at least twice Kayla's age, and he wasn't convinced that a young person, and a 'woman' at that, had the capability to efficiently manage his wealth that 'he had slaved so hard to create.'

The Dragon knew that DMC Wealth Management was the most reputable wealth management firm in the California area, because of the caliber of their clientele, their team of wealth managers and advisors were advanced, versed and above par and they were famous for the reputation of making millionaires and multi-millionaires into billionaires. And it was this reputation that attracted the multi-millionaire Alistair Ortega, a.k.a. 'The Dragon' to DMC Wealth. His portfolio was assigned to Kayla and she was going above and beyond to prove to him that she was more than capable of managing his wealth, but he was hard to convince.

He had given Kayla a three-month trial period to prove him wrong, and unknown to him she had exceeded his expectations before the test period. She had decided to take it a little further and triple what he had allowed her to invest.

By the end of the month (the test period), she would be ready to silence 'The Dragon' for good. However, even though he gave Kayla a test period, that didn't stop him from calling every Thursday to follow up on her progress. He ranted on how certain he was that the promises she had made on his portfolio gain, within the three months, would be impossible and ludicrous.

The sound of the incoming video call tone from the Skype app on Kayla's computer, alerted her that 'The Dragon' was calling. She took a deep breath, rocked her head from side to side, managed to form her lips into a bright, confident smile and answered the call.

She groaned inwardly. This was going to be a long three hours. Despite her bright smile, she knew any contact with him would leave a dark rain cloud that would no doubt hover over the rest of her day.

At half past one, James walked into Café Délice and sat at a table in the back facing the door where he would see Kayla the moment she walked in. He was nervous to say the least, he must have gone through the discussion he was planning to have with Kayla over a thousand times in his head...and every time he imagined that she would believe him, forgive him and they would both find a way to deal with Elizabeth. But, in the back of his mind he was realistic and he knew he had to prepare for the total opposite of what he expected to happen.

At 1:45 p.m, Kayla approached the Café. he suddenly got very awkward; he tried to sit up straight, ran his hands through his hair, looked down on his shirt, he really couldn't help the way he started to feel or behave, and she wasn't even in front of him yet!

As Kayla entered the Café and looked around, James was already up walking towards her. He signaled and the moment she saw him she froze, a cloud settled over her face as she realized his ploy.

Kayla scrunched her face, annoyed and pissed that James was

the one trying to waste her time. She quickly started to make her way out of the Café.

"Kayla wait!" James shouted as he ran after her. "Please just hear me out, you need to hear what I have to say, you may be in danger..."

She was already outside of the Café, on the street corridor when he caught up to her. He held on to her hand and tried to stop her but she wouldn't have it.

"You have some nerve James!" she said angrily turning around to face him. "What do you think was going to happen? You lied to get me here and then I would what... just sit down and chat...what do you want...?"

"Kayla, I swear, this is not a personal agenda." James pleaded with a sincere and desperate look on his face. "...I – I just need ten minutes of your time, I wouldn't have gone to this trouble if it wasn't important...and we both know if I didn't lie you wouldn't have willingly met with me."

"Please, let's just go inside, once I tell you what I have to say you can leave, please..."

Kayla looked at him with hate-filled eyes.

Other diners sitting on the outside corridor of the café stared at them and she felt a bit embarrassed. "You—have—ten—minutes" she minced out the words as if they were smeared with bile. She strode past him back into the café. James quickly followed and as he walked past her to the table, he tried to pull out a chair for her to sit. She grabbed the back of the chair, rejecting his gesture and pulled it out herself.

James went around to the next chair and sat down. "Look Kayla…" he said, trying to make eye contact with her. "…I know I lied to get you here but it's for a good reason…you may be in danger."

"Danger?" Kayla asked with a sarcastic laugh. "Is that the best you could come up with? Ok James if I'm in 'danger' as you put it, I presume you are my knight-in-shining-armor here to save me? Please James, don't waste my time, just tell me the real reason why you tricked me into coming here."

James was about to answer when a waitress walked over to take their order. "Just get me some coffee for now." James said to the waitress trying to hurry her away.

"I'll have an orange wine spritzer please" Kayla said to her. "I'm going to need a drink to get me through this…" she mumbled under her breath. The waitress took their orders and left.

James heard what she had muttered and continued to speak. "Look Kayla…I know I'm the last person you want to see right now and regardless of what you think of me, I wouldn't have put you in this situation if it wasn't of utmost importance."

Kayla rolled her eyes at him. She would be a darn fool to believe anything that was coming out of his mouth. "Elizabeth is not who she is pretending to be with you…" James said leaning closer to Kayla.

"This is what this is about?" Kayla said looking and sounding even more annoyed, and cutting James off before he could finish "…My relationship with your ex-wife is the danger I'm in? Oh James, I'm convinced you are sick in the head…I need to go. I won't listen to another word that comes out of your mouth."

"For God sakes Kayla just listen to me!" James said in a slightly raised, stern tone that redirected Kayla's attention. This commanding aspect of his character that Kayla had loved very much, a part of him that would only come out in the bedroom, often rendered her helpless and speechless. She would not show him how he affected her so she stilled and glared at him.

"Elizabeth is the reason you are here in California," James continued. "I don't know the details of how she did it, but I know she has major influence in your company because she sits on the advisory board of directors there."

James could see in Kayla's eyes that he had gotten her attention but that she was also confused by what he was saying.

"Look Kayla," he continued "...from the moment I found out that you were the one Elizabeth was with, I knew it was no coincidence and I suspected that she had something up her sleeves. She came over to my house on Tuesday to get something she had left behind and I confronted her about her relationship with you, and about my suspicions. At first, she tried to deny it, telling me that it was purely coincidence the way you both met. But I didn't believe her and so I pushed her a little further; she practically admitted that she's using you in her sick plans to destroy me... 'To leave me with nothing' were her exact words. She even suggested that she was going to propose to you, which I suspect is her way of keeping you bound to her while she perfects her plans."

At James mention of the proposal, Kayla's heart dropped and she held on to her hand with the ring, which directed James eyes to look down on her finger.

"Oh God…" James said, swallowing convulsively while staring at the ring. "She wasn't lying, she already proposed." He noted with a gleam of satisfaction, that in response, Kayla downed the remainder of her wine spritzer in one big gulp. She had been sipping on the drink all along. This was his opening to press his point home. "…I believe she has a hand in your transfer from Vancouver to California," James said carefully, imbuing his words with the strength he knew that she liked about him. "My friend Brad is also on the board at your company and he says Elizabeth has the power to make those calls."

"She can't be on the board…" Kayla said, her voice trailing off. "I have met with all the board members on more than one occasion and she was never there…so that cannot be true…." She shook her head as if to re-orient herself with the reality she knew.

"My friend Brad says she keeps herself anonymous to the rest of the organization and only converse with the CEO and other managing partners, much like her dad did before he died."

"Who is this Brad you keep referring to…how does he claim to know so much?" Kayla asked with a hint of doubt.

"His name is Bradley Axton," James replied evenly. "But I call him Brad, his dad is…"

Before James could finish the sentence, Kayla interjected, "Keith Axton…?"

"Yes," James confirmed. "Do you know him?

"I do…" Kayla replied, "Keith stepped down from the board last month and was replaced by his son Bradley… I only know him by his full name; Bradley Axton, and that is why I didn't know who you were referring to when you said Brad. So, he's the one who told you all this about Elizabeth being on the board...but why?"

"He helped me to secure this meeting with you," James replied. "He was more so trying to find out why I wasn't asking my 'wife' Elizabeth, to get me the meeting since she was a prominent member on the board. Before I had that conversation with Brad, I had absolutely no clue that Elizabeth had ties in wealth management...that shows you how much I really know about my wife, she hid this away from me all these years and I was supposed to be her husband, I'm telling you Kayla she cannot be trusted."

"This is all so much to process all at once," Kayla said, gulping down her fourth wine spritzer. "Why would Elizabeth have me transferred here, what does she want from me?" Raw doubt seemed to be festering and her face was looking pensive.

He could not stop now, he had to cement the doubts in her mind. "I don't know exactly what she wants Kayla, but I know she is up to no good. I know she has plans to use you in some way to hurt me but exactly how I don't know."

Kayla raised her hand up, like a stop-sign. "For all we know, this could all be a coincidence James," Kayla interjected, hanging on to her faith in Liz but doubt etched its way across her features. "It makes no sense; how can she use me to hurt you? You made it clear in the way you left that I meant nothing to you. I have nothing to do with the lies you told your wife all those years. So, if she's seeking revenge, why bring me into it when she knows

I never knew you were married, when she knows that I am as much as a victim as she is." Kayla breathed hard trying to collect herself. "Why should I even believe anything you say, for all I know you could just be using these coincidences to weasel your way back into my heart? Why are you only telling me this now when you had other opportunities...?"

"Other opportunities..." James cut her off, sounding confused, "Kayla what are you talking about?"

She threw him a disparaging glance, rolling her eyes. "I'm talking about the Stargazer lilies you sent to my office...with the note, *"I miss you...Love James"*, which obviously means you know where I work. And, if all this is true, the moment you suspected Elizabeth as you claimed, you could have approached me then... months ago...why wait until now...when we are engaged...the more I think about it, the more I think that you are the one lying and we both know you are great at that".

The expression on James face painted his innocence and confused state. "Kayla, I swear to you I never sent you Stargazer lilies since you came to California. I only sent you those lilies when you were back in Vancouver and I couldn't be there. This is news to me...when did you get them?"

"James, you are the only one who knows that Stargazer Lilies are my favorite and the note says, *"Love James"*—are you really going to deny that you sent them. Are you going to say Elizabeth sent them?"

"Who else?" James asked, his expression begging for Kayla to believe him, "Elizabeth may know more about you than you think she does... and it's for this reason why I'm begging you to believe me." He stared, unwaveringly, into her eyes without guile. "I didn't send those flowers Kayla, because before yesterday, other than the fact that you were with Elizabeth, I knew nothing else of what you were doing here in California, I didn't even know where you were working." He cupped his shoulders and rubbed the kinks out of his shoulders and neck. As Shakespeare, in *Hamlet*, says, 'something is rotten in the State of Denmark', and by God, James was going to get to the bottom of this. His and Kayla's futures may depend on it. He locked gaze with Kayla again and said, "When Elizabeth failed to deny that she had a hand with you being here, that's when I knew I had to do everything in my power to let you know what she was up to. I called your old office back in Vancouver and spoke to your former boss, Matthew Perez—that's how I found out where you worked — just yesterday." He saw doubt gathering new clouds on her face. "You can call him and confirm if you don't believe me. I swear to you, everything I did back then and risk doing now is because I love you."

She sprang back from him as if she was stung. He hastened to explain. "Kayla, I ended our relationship the way I did because I had no choice. Elizabeth threatened to find you and ruin your life if I didn't..." He pursed his lips and glanced away, into the painful past. "... Back then, I knew she knew I was in another relationship with someone in Vancouver but I never knew she had any idea who it was. But I know my wife, and I knew she had the resources to find you if she wanted to. I was sloppy, I left credit card trails that had addresses of the places I bought the gifts that I sent to you whenever I was away, and she found them all." His hands visibly shook and he ran them through the sides of his hair in an effort to still them. His voice turned tremulous. "I knew it would have been only a matter of time until she would find you if I didn't break things off. Plus, the fact that she also threatened to take my children away from me."

Kayla's face was tight like a mask. Her eyes darted about the restaurant as if seeking a truth other than what was being presented.

James knew he was gaining ground with Kayla and pressed on, even though she was avoiding his eyes. She was listening as he continued. "My marriage with Elizabeth was honestly on the rocks when I met you, but I had my daughter Charlotte to think about. I knew what a divorce could do to her so I erased the thought from my mind despite my better judgement. And that's the only reason I could not have been honest with you back then. Be honest Kayla, would you have given me the light of day if I had told you the truth? To be honest when we first started out I didn't know where our relationship was going to go...and I had no reason to confide in you about what was really going on in my life, which made lying to you so much easier." Unconsciously, he slipped into *The Thinker Pose*, except that his elbow rested on the table instead of his knee. "Before I knew it our relationship had blossomed into everything I had ever wanted in a relationship and I had fallen in love with you deeper than I could have ever imagined I would." His voice suddenly sounded very tired and world-weary. "I thought about coming clean with you...I really did...but by then you had loved me as much or even more than I had loved you. You trusted me, and I lied for so long that I feared that if I told you the truth I would have lost you."

Kayla stared down at her drink, her fingers sliding up and down the sides of her glass, wiping the beads of moisture away as quickly as they formed. Yet her body was still. Listening.

James sipped on his now cold coffee, giving him pause to continue his recollection: "When I left Vancouver and returned to California in that two-year period, when I lied to you that my brother was getting a divorce, I really left because Elizabeth had found out and had threatened to divorce me and take Charlotte away from me." He beckoned to the waiter to replenish his coffee and refill Kayla's drink. After the waiter left, he reached out to touch her hand but instead balled it into a fist. It wasn't time yet. Distrust was too high right now. His spirit somehow began to lift as he needed to make her understand. He spoke softly—almost in a whisper: "I love my daughter Kayla and could not let what was going on between Elizabeth and I ruin her life...I—I—went back to be there for my daughter." His voice cracked. "Things got even more complicated with Elizabeth when I went back, but because I had you in my life I managed to live through my nightmare of a marriage."

Kayla rolled her eyes but he could see a thin veil of moisture welling up.

He told her, "Elizabeth had succeeded in getting me back to California but she knew I was no longer in love with her... and that did not sit well with her...so when she found out that I was still seeing you even though I was back with her, she went berserk on me"

Kayla chuckled, without any mirth. "Well, do you blame her, dealing with a player?"

James ignored her question, determined to get his story out. "Kayla, just hear me out. Anyway, she redrafted every paperwork regarding our marriage and my ties in the company, she made it so that if she ever caught me cheating again she could divorce me and I would get nothing. She went as far as drugging me so that she could sleep with me to have our second child David, because she knew Charlotte was the only reason I stayed, because I didn't care about her wealth, I had my own dreams. And so, she used her pregnancy with David to draw me closer to her and to trap me in California for those two years."

"But even then, I never stopped loving you. I never ended our relationship and that was when Elizabeth made the threat against your life. I had no choice but to end it. She went as far as to sell the properties and close the businesses we had in Vancouver. She made me do the dirty work of explaining to the hundreds of people we employed back in Vancouver, why we had to let them go. When I came back Kayla, I wanted nothing more than to stay with you, I wanted nothing more than to tell you the truth, but it wouldn't have mattered, you would have hated me anyway for lying to you in the first place."

"You are right about that. What was that poem from high school?

Black is Black
White is White
And a lie is never the truth

"Kayla…" James sighed. "I deserve it all because I lied to you in the first place. I had to end it with you because over the years I had seen what Elizabeth was capable of. She had evolved into someone that I was scared of. She had completely changed from the woman I had fallen in love with and had married. And because of that, as much as I wanted to be with you, I couldn't live with myself if I allowed her to hurt you."

Kayla snickered. "So, you were protecting me."

"I was! I ended things the way I did with you because I intentionally wanted you to hate me. I thought that if I ended our relationship that way you would never want anything to do with me ever again, and so I wouldn't get tempted to come back to you... I did it so that you would be safe. I admit that I was selfish in taking you to the lake and making you feel that everything was ok, but I wanted to have that one last memory with you. I had always planned to propose to you and the thought that the cabin would be gone and I would never again get the chance, I acted out of pure selfishness. And I took you there, made you believe I was going to propose just so you could see how perfect it would be...and for that I'm sorry. I swear to you, I have never stopped loving you. For once in my life I am being totally honest with you...I did what I did to protect you"

Kayla smothered a sound that was a cross between a laugh and a sob. "Why should I believe you now James...everything you have ever told me were lies? What makes this time any different...you know what...just don't answer that."

Kayla looked away from James with a sliver of pain in her eyes, she wanted so badly to believe James, but it was just too much to take in. Elizabeth had told her a different version of the story and now James was telling his version and she honestly didn't know who to believe. James read it all over her face.

"I never sent those lilies to your office Kayla," James said trying to make his case. "I believe Elizabeth did, and if she did, she is trying to test you, to see if you are still in love with me. She may have sent them to you and then unsuspectingly asked you about it in a casual conversation to see if you would be honest with her. She has played that game with me many times."

"Come to think of it..." Kayla said, as she recalled the conversation she and Liz had that night over dinner. "She did ask me if there was 'anything out of the ordinary' that happened at work that day... I thought she was just trying to make conversation. But now it seems like she was really fishing for me to tell her about the flowers, because I told her something else and she asked again, emphasizing if there was anything else."

James was sure of what he was telling Kayla and he could see that she was starting to put it together for herself though still hesitant. He knew Kayla wanted to believe everything he had said but she couldn't deny that she had doubts. He couldn't blame her. He had lied to her for so many years that she found it extremely difficult to separate the truth from the lies in his argument.

"I don't know what to believe anymore," Kayla said in a bewildered tone. Why do these things keep happening to me...why does it seems like everywhere I turn I'm being used, lied to and deceived?" Her voice shook with the effort it took to stem the flow of tears that were now running down her cheeks.

James reached for her hand and tried to console her, but she pulled away... "I can't do this now James, I just can't, I need to wrap my head around all this, I need time to think, I need time to decide who is really telling the truth...I just need to get away from you both."

"Kayla you can't let Elizabeth know that you are having doubts. You can't let her know that I told you any of this. She cannot know that you met with me. When I confronted her at my house she made it clear that if I interfered in any way to turn your mind against her, there's no telling what she would do to you."

"Look..." he said, swallowing hard, his Adam's Apple visibly shifting up and down. "...I know this is a lot to process, and I am not asking you to take my word for it. I'm just asking you to look into what I have told you, look into her ties with your company, look into the flowers you received because I know I didn't send them. Be perceptive of Elizabeth, use her own tactics against her to try and get the information you need. You need to be a step ahead of her in whatever she is planning. But please, I'm begging you, don't alert her suspicions. Don't draw attention to yourself while you try to uncover the truth. Just carry on like you normally would. When you find out that what I'm saying is the truth, which I'm sure you will, just give me a call and we can decide then what to do." James then pulled a card from his wallet with his cell number and gave it to Kayla.

Kayla got up from her chair, she looked at James wanting to say something but she just didn't know what to say. She was experiencing more emotions at once that she wouldn't in a million years thought she could.

James placed the money in the holder containing the bill that the waitress had left and then got up with Kayla. She walked ahead of him in the direction of the door. When she got outside she turned to him and said. "You know…. I may never have stayed with you back then if you had told me the truth, but I would have waited for you while you sorted yourself out. Fast-forward to now, the truth would have made this situation so much easier and probably we would not be in the situation we are in now. It's like you said James, you were selfish, selfish to my feelings, selfish for wasting so many years of my life as an escape from your so called 'terrible marriage.' And for that, I don't think I can ever truly forgive you…no matter what your reasons were. Kayla dropped his card in her purse then slipped on her shades and walked away.

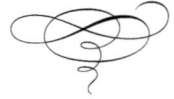

Chapter 14

That evening Kayla went home late, she sat in her office for hours after work just going over all James had told her. She questioned herself that if it was all true, why her...why did she have to meet James in the first place?

Why did it seem that every chance she has gotten at love has all been based on lies and deception?

Why did it seem as if the universe was punishing her for something she knew nothing about?

She was staying with Liz that evening and while she sat in the office late trying to avoid facing Liz knowing all she did, she knew she had to go. She couldn't alert Liz's suspicions as James had warned, so she packed up her things and headed home to Liz with the plan that she would just tell Liz that she had a long day and go straight to bed.

On Friday morning, Kayla woke up before her alarm went off. It was more so that she really couldn't sleep and spent the entire night lying motionless beside Liz, praying for morning to come so she could leave. She wanted nothing more than to confront her, to get the truth.

It was nearly 4 am when she woke up and Liz was not beside her. She stumbled to the bathroom; her eyes still foggy from lack of sleep. She splashed water on her face and brushed her teeth. As she was about to step into the shower, she heard whispering chatter coming from the next room.

Was that Liz whispering? About to call out, Kayla abruptly changed her mind and instead silently walked from the bedroom to the corridor adjacent to the room that the whispers were coming from. Kayla stood outside the bedroom door and quickly realized that Liz was on the phone. She couldn't help but wonder who Liz was speaking to in hushed tones at 4 am. She tried her hardest to listen closely to what Liz was saying. What she heard had her entire body paralyzed with shock and fear. She began to hyperventilate as she listened.

Bernard, it was my family's money and influence that got you to where you are today. Do you believe that you would have ever been made CEO of DMC Wealth without my anonymous votes and influence, and not to mention the pockets I had to fill to make it all happen? This means that you owe me big time... and I am not done cashing in my favors just yet."

"...I know what I said Bernard you don't need to remind me, but now that she is here there is one more thing I need from you. I had you assign Alistair Ortega's portfolio to Kayla for a reason...Alistair is a miserable and paranoid old fart who won't hesitate to bury her the moment he finds out that she has been investing his money illegally and stealing from his portfolio..."

"I know she is not actually stealing or investing his money illegally Bernard...I'm saying I want you to make it look like she is. I want you to override her access to his accounts, just long enough to remove the funds from Alistair investment portfolio, and make it seem as if she lost all his money investing in some Ponzi schemes."

"I have created an offshore account in her name. I want you to send a portion of the funds, maybe twelve million dollars from Alistair's account to the offshore account. I'll send you the details of the account as soon as I hang up. I want you to do this now Bernard, before she gets into work. If you had answered your phone when I called you yesterday, I wouldn't need to be calling you this early."

"I'll send an anonymous tip to Alistair about the suspected misuse of his funds, and him being as paranoid as he is, will immediately launch an investigation. He calls her every Thursday, so I'll get the tip to him by next Wednesday. Listen Bernard, on the surface I want every-thing to look normal, make it so that whenever she accesses the account she'll suspect nothing; it will only be revealed when the investigation is launched next Thursday and by then it would have been too late for her to do anything about it. She'll be indicted and the evidence will be so overwhelming that she'll spend the rest of her miserable life in Jail."

"...And what about the company's reputation Bernard...you worry too much...We will still have Alistair's money so we will pay him back everything and even more so that the company's name is omitted from the slander. I'll pay the press if I have to make sure the focus is on Kayla only...and not the company...trust me this is not my first rodeo."

"Just do what needs to be done on your end and leave the rest to me... she'll never know what's coming to hit her...I have to go...call me later when it's all done...bye."

At the obvious end of Liz's phone conversation, Kayla managed to get a hold of herself long enough to silently run back to the bedroom and get in the shower. Body shaking, she quickly slipped off her silk night gown and tossed it over the shower door before she turned on the faucet.

Shortly after, she could hear Liz walking into the bedroom. No way could she give an inkling that she had overheard the conversation. She had to think fast…play it cool.

"Liz is that you darling," she asked, disguising the fear and nervousness that had taken hold of her body.

Liz paused before answering… "Yes, it's me…" she answered, "…I couldn't sleep so I went to the kitchen to make some warm milk….should I get some for you?"

"No…that's OK." Kayla answered keeping up the pretense. "…I got up early so I can get ready and stop by my apartment before I get to work…I left some files there that I'm going to need for a meeting today, so I have to get a head start if I want to make it in on time".

"That's fine…" Liz replied; since I'm already up, I'm just going to go out for a jog. Will I be seeing you tonight?"

"Aaah…sure…," Kayla responded hesitantly. "…I'll let you know if there's any change of plans…I love you…"

"I love you too," Liz responded, as she slipped into her running gear. Do have a great day," and she left.

Once Kayla could no longer hear Liz inside the room, she turned off the water and held onto her chest, releasing the backup of panting breaths that she had held to disguise what she was really feeling.

She fell to her knees inside the bathtub and curled herself up into a ball, holding onto her feet for dear life and her head buried on the top of her knees.

And she cried.

It was happening all over again, it was all true. Liz didn't love her, it was no coincidence how they met, it was planned. Once again, she had fallen for the lies and the deception and it burned her heart like an open flame on skin.

Oh, how she had wished that what James had insinuated about Liz wasn't true.

But it was, and it was staring her right in the face, she heard right. Liz was speaking to Bernard, the CEO of DMC Wealth. Liz was planning to ruin her life, her career, and send her to jail for embezzlement and fraud and it seemed that there was nothing she could do about it.

She was panicking, thoughts bombarded her head so much so that she thought it was going to explode. She grabbed her head with both hands and screamed.

She stood up and stepped out of the shower, she could no longer feel sorry for herself…she had to find a way to stop this, there had to be a way out.

She grabbed a towel from the towel rack and dried her body. Twisting her hair into a bun she dashed to the bedroom to get dressed. How she looked didn't matter, she quickly slipped into a slip dress she had in her overnight bag, grabbed her phone, and purse and sailed out the door.

On her way to her apartment she called Lisa from the car. "Lisa, please, I need you to clear my calendar for today. I have an emergency situation to attend to and I don't know what time I'll be able to make it to the office. If anyone calls or ask for me, tell them *I'm working out of the office today.* Call me if you need me." After she hung up, she took a few deep breaths. She hoped she didn't sound too frantic so that Lisa could alert Bernard as to her state of mind. She had to stay sane.

Where was James' card? She rummaged through her pocketbook, looking through the different compartments where she had carelessly tossed it. When she found it, she clutched it for dear life. She called him.

"James its Kayla."

"Kayla I'm so glad you called, I think I've figured out how we can find out what Elizabeth is planning…" James responded; but before he could finish Kayla interjected.

"I need you to come to my place now. I'll text you the address as soon as I hang up and I'll explain everything once you get there; please hurry."

After she hung up, it was as if she couldn't drive fast enough to get home. She sped through two yellow lights. Breathe…, breathe… she kept telling herself. At the next red light, she quickly texted James her address.

A few minutes later she pulled up to her driveway, she hopped out of the car and without even making sure it was locked she grabbed her bag and keys and ran inside the house. In the living room, she paced back and forth, waiting for James to show-up. Meanwhile, her future flashed before her eyes…the accusations…the guilty verdict…the end of her career … her life in prison. Oh God, her father. This will surely kill him.

Within twenty minutes, a welcoming knock resounded on her door. It was James and she flung the door open. James walked in, searching her wan face for a preview of what was to come. Her hands trembled and her eyes revealed stark terror. "I came as soon as you called," he said. "What's going on. What has she done?"

"It is all true…" Kayla said, pacing around the room. "Everything you suspected about her…it's all true. My promotion to DMC California, using me, planning to ruin my life, my career, it's all true," She stifled a sob, tears blinding her and she felt for the sofa to sit on.

James was dumbfounded, more so because he was worried that Kayla may have confronted Elizabeth for the information she now knew and he was afraid of what was going to come next.

James sat down next to her on the sofa.

"How do you know all this…how did you confirm it…" James asked.

"I heard her…I heard her on the phone this morning with Bernard…" Kayla responded with her eyes staring past James as she recollect Liz's conversation.

"Who is Bernard?" James asked, trying to understand.

"Bernard is my boss here in California, he is the CEO of DMC Wealth…he is the one who came to Vancouver and spoke to Matthew about promoting me. And this morning I just found out that he is working for Elizabeth, or at least that's how it sounded."

James had a look on his face that told Kayla he wanted her to complete the story for it to completely sink in, so she continued.

"I got up early this morning, earlier than I normally would because I just couldn't sleep. Everything that you told me yesterday—about Liz, about you, it weighed on me all night and I just couldn't sleep. "I thought I'd just get up early and leave for the office so I could have time to figure out what to do next. But James, when I woke up I realized she wasn't in bed."

"Where did she go?"

"I didn't think anything of it—I was about to get into the shower when I heard whispers coming from the next bedroom."

"I tiptoed and stood by the door, and it was Elizabeth on the phone. At first, she sounded like she was angry at someone, but as I listened further, it became clear to me that the conversation was about me, and that she was talking to the CEO of DMC."

"What?" James mouth gaped in shock.

"It was clear he had owed her favors because apparently it was her money and connections that made him CEO of the company. What she said made it clear that she was also the one who had me promoted to California, by using Bernard to carry out the hire. She has somehow gotten Bernard to assign me a client that I have been working with for some months now..., she plans to empty this clients account; where they'll launder some of the money into an offshore account that she has established in my name and the rest will be made to appear as if I invested in some Ponzi scheme."

James face turned white as an Easter lily. He was breathing hard.

"She's planning to ruin my life James. She is planning to have me indicted for embezzlement and fraud, I'll go to prison for years if not for the rest of my life, for something I never did!" she sobbed as tears ran down her face.

"And the worst part about it...I have no proof...what do I tell the police? All of the fraudulent transactions will be in my name...the laundered money will be in an offshore account in my name. If I go to the police it will be her word against mine. And we both know I have no proof, plus she'll have Bernard to confirm it and testify against me. James I'll be doomed to spend the rest of my life in prison. Oh God....I'll be finished," she wailed.

With the shock of what Kayla had just told him, James got up to his feet and staggered a bit before he could firmly plant his feet. He knew Elizabeth was up to something...but he could never have guessed that it was something of this magnitude.

"No....no...no..." he shouted with one hand fixed to the side of his head. "Jesus Christ Elizabeth...who are you?"

"She's a monster that's who she is," Kayla said, standing on her feet, tears still flowing down her face. I have done nothing to deserve this." She pointed an accusatory finger at James letting loose a flow of disjointed diatribe. "You lied your way into my life James, you deceived me into believing you were mine all those years...and I told her all this—the minute I found out who she was." I—I— was honest with her...and she lied to me ...when we first met, she pretended to have no idea of who I was.... When I told her about you, she pretended to understand... She made me believe it was ok—when all along she knew everything—all along she was planning to ruin my life...despite having all the facts."

James pulled her closer to his chest. "Shhh… calm down. Let's strategize.

Kayla was at the point of no return, spewing her anger, and troubled state of mind. "She deceived me into falling in love with her…all so that she could pull me closer and get the information she needed to ruin my life…she is a monster…you both are…all you both do is lie and deceive and hurt the people you claim you love…this is all your fault!"

Kayla broke down even more and she started to hit James repeatedly as she sobbed. All the hate and frustration she had held back when she had confronted him months ago was all coming out at that moment.

James could not speak, because he too had blamed himself for the situation she was in and the way he deceived her all those years. He held her hands to slow down her blows, pulling her closer to him, hugging her…holding on to her tight as she broke down. He had to do something. His heart bled. Elizabeth had finally succeeded in hurting him in the worst way she knew how—by hurting the one he truly loved.

"Kayla please…" he said, holding her head with both hands and looking into her eyes. I know it is easier said than done… but you have to compose yourself…we'll figure this out. When is Elizabeth planning to falsify the evidence against you?"

Kayla released herself from James grip and dabbed at her eyes to check the flow of tears. "They plan on alerting Alistair, my client of the 'fraud' next Wednesday so that he'll enact the investigation by Thursday. So, by then I'll be under investigation and taken into custody the same day. What am I going to do…I have no proof to vindicate myself!"

James slowly paced the room, deep in thought. "I don't think that is entirely true Kayla."

Kayla's head snapped to attention, "What?"

"Remember I was trying to tell you that I think I might have a way of figuring out what Elizabeth is planning? Well I do. It's a long shot…but if I'm right, I think it will be your evidence against Elizabeth, to prove that she is trying to frame you."

"What are you talking about?" Kayla asked looking slightly confused.

James stopped pacing and took her hand. "Let's sit down and come up with a strategy." She obediently sat, but on the edge of her seat. James eased himself down to sit next to her. He held her hand and this time she didn't flinch. After a short pause to collect his thoughts he said, "after a conversation I had with an old law school friend of mine, who also knew Elizabeth back then, he made me realize that Elizabeth was as callous as she is now from the moment I had met her…I just wasn't able to see it because I was in love with her. That conversation led me to really think…really try and find clues in our past—earlier on in our marriage that I may have ignored…clues I could use to really understand the type of woman I had married."

"And …?" Kayla asked wearily.

"And that's when it hit me…in the second year of our marriage, I came across a journal that Elizabeth kept in her underwear drawer."

"Oh? And so …" Kayla said with impatience.

"I had only scanned through it then, because the journal had such an intriguing look. I wasn't intentionally trying to invade her privacy, but I can vaguely remember that there was a passage in it that caught my attention. It had something to do with some steps taken to blacklist someone that had gotten in the way of the black widow."

"The black widow," Kayla intoned, trying to grasp where he was going with this.

"When I think back, the steps sounded exactly like what my friend Asher said happened to Ava Murano, a girl that was interested in me back in Law school while I was dating Elizabeth. Back then it made no sense, because I had no clue she was threatened by Ava. And I had no clue she had taken unspeakable actions to get rid of Ava. But now I understand perfectly."

Kayla was still looking a bit lost—she couldn't exactly understand how what James was saying applied in any way to her situation.

"Don't you see?" James gushed. "Elizabeth keeps a journal of all her horrendous deeds…in the journal she refers to herself as the black widow, which is one of the reasons I never figured it out back then that what she wrote was actually what she had done to Ava." I believe she still keeps that journal, and if you find it, chances are she would have detailed all that she has planned against you in it."

"A journal," Kayla repeated with a 'deer in headlights' stare. That's gonna save me…a journal."

"It's a long shot but it's a start, and it is definitely worth a try if it means we'll find proof of her plans against you. It is tangible evidence that we could give to the police to warrant a proper investigation that will vindicate you if it ever comes to that."

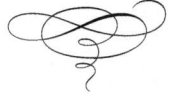

Chapter 15

Kayla sat back down and tried to fathom what James told her. "How would I even get close to her underwear drawer to supposedly find this journal with her in the house?"

"You need to do it when she is not there," James responded. "Today is Friday, she usually goes to the farmers market on Tuesdays and Fridays...that means she'll be going today. She usually goes around midday...around that time you need to call her to confirm that's she's not home....let it seem as if you are just casually checking on how her day is going...then you need to go to the house and find that journal."

Kayla did not like this one bit. Her head was spinning with the turn of events. Her entire world was topsy-turvy and her heart ached with loss and the details of this deception.

James gave her a sympathetic glance and spoke in a gentler tone. "As it is right now, the hope is that Liz would have implicated herself by logging in that journal how she plans to frame you. It is the only proof I can think of that will truly work in your favor. In the meantime, I'm going to speak with my friend Bradley. Maybe if I explain the situation hypothetically, he might be able to give me some suggestions on how to stop it before it occurs."

"And how would he be able to do that?" Kayla asked doubtfully.

"I don't know, I'm guessing since he has a strong advisory background with your company he may have come across a few situations of internal fraud and how to deal with it. I'm guessing a man of his caliber has to know something or someway to prevent these things...I don't know Kayla...I'm just throwing out suggestions here and it doesn't hurt to try. We need to stop Elizabeth before she strikes and we're going to need all the help and advice we can get."

Kayla shook her head in agreement, her face sagged with worry as she absently stared at the abstract painting on the wall.

"Look..." James continued. "I know you feel helpless. I do too, but I promise you we can get through this together. I will not sit back and let her ruin your life for something I started. I'll die trying to save you from her clutches if it's the last thing I do.

He tilted her chin around to face him. "So, we need to act fast, act smart and not draw attention to ourselves. Will you be going to work as usual?"

"I can't go to work James...with all that's going on that is the last place I want to be. I've already contacted my personal assistant Lisa, I told her if anyone asked, I'm working out of the office today. Its's not unusual—so I don't think there's anything to worry about. I'll just stay here until it's time to confirm that Liz is not at the house and then I'll go look for the journal.

Besides, I'm closer to her house here than if I was at the office. I can act faster in getting in and out before she returns."

James agreed and kissed her on the forehead before he hesitantly left the house. Kayla went to her bedroom and slid into something that she felt more comfortable in...and then she went to the kitchen and made some tea that took her forever to drink as she had no appetite for anything.

She glanced over at her phone on the kitchen counter for the time and it was 9:45 am. She calculated that she had another hour or so before she had to make the dreaded call to Elizabeth to confirm her whereabouts before heading to the house.

She went back to the living room and checked her purse to ensure that she had taken the set of keys Liz had made for her. Yes, she had them. With nothing else to do but wait the remaining hour seemed like a lifetime.

She sat on the couch twiddling with her fingers, and every now and then glancing at her phone for the time. After some time had passed, she glanced over again and the time was 11:52 a.m., she thought it was a perfect time to call. If James was right Elizabeth wouldn't be home.

She cleared her throat and picked up the phone. She took a deep breath to compose herself and to smooth out the croaks that her sessions of crying had left in her voice.

She scrolled down the 'recent' call logs in her phone and called Liz's number.

Liz answered in a rather cheery voice and it made Kayla cringe at the thought of how coldblooded she really was.

"Hey..." Kayla said in response to Liz's cheery greeting. "I'm just checking in on you—since we didn't have a chance to really speak this morning."

"How's your day going..." Kayla tried to perk up her voice.

"I'm actually at the grocery store ..." Liz replied. It's pretty much an errand day for me today..." she continued. Remember the kids officially move in tomorrow, so I'm out getting their favorites. Charlotte loves strawberries so I'll be stopping by the farmers market after the grocery store... then to the winery for something for the adults..." she giggled. "That's pretty much how I'll be spending my day for the most part. How about you?"

"My day is pretty much like yours," Kayla replied. "Only, instead of errands, I have a ton of client meetings to attend... but don't let me bore you with my day...I just wanted to hear your voice. I'll see you later...I love you...bye."

As soon as Kayla hung up she grabbed her purse and keys from the dining table and hurried to her car. The grocery store wasn't far from Liz's house and neither was the farmers market....she had to make her way there immediately if she was to get in and out before Liz returned.

She arrived at the house in less than thirty minutes, thanks to how fast she was driving, she jumped out of her car leaving the engine running. Filled with jumbled nerves, her hands fumbled with the keys in the door lock before she could get it open.

With hopes that she would find the journal, with the evidence, she dashed up the staircase, tripping before she got to the top from the nervousness that had taken over her body.

She managed to quickly rise and continued to Liz's bedroom. Opening the top drawer of the dresser, she anxiously rummaged through Liz's delicates but the journal was not there. She went through the remaining four drawers but still she couldn't seem to find the journal.

Panic bloomed with short, panting breaths and her chest constricted. Where could the journal be? What if it had proof of Liz's plot to frame her?[It was her only chance. She took a deep breath trying to compose herself. She tried to think, where she would keep such a diary if she ever had one, if she was in Liz's shoe.

Somewhere private she thought...somewhere the person you were plotting against would not think to look...somewhere out of sight.

She ran downstairs to Liz's study, she immediately went to her office desk. The first drawer had nothing more than papers and folders. She closed it and tried to open the second drawer but it was locked. Desperately she jiggled it but it wouldn't open. She needed a key... she stood still for a moment...out of options of what to do.

She ran to the kitchen and grabbed a butter knife and ran back to Liz's study. She got on her knees and pushed the tip of the butter knife into the lock...twisting it from side to side...it took some time for the knife to manipulate the inside of the lock before it popped open.

She opened the drawer...and there it was...the journal. The cover was made from dark brown leather with a peculiar sculpture protruding from the center of the cover.

Kayla opened the lock of the journal and began to flip through the pages, using the dates and the headings as a guide to what she was looking for. All the while she was hoping and praying, anxious to find what she was anticipating would be there.

She came upon a few pages that she just could not flip by… they were unbelievable…she quickly realized that the person she was dealing with was demented, psychotic, and dangerous.

Stunned, she learned that Liz had murdered her father in the most obscure way and the fact that she had lost no sleep over the atrocities she had committed made Kayla fear even more for her own life.

Another page made it clear to her of the reasons why James had tried to run away from Liz…what she was trying to do to him was unbelievable.

As she got closer to the more recent dates, she quickly realized that her own downfall was planned for as long as she was with James. And as she got closer to the current dates, her heart skipped. She had found what she was looking for.

It was all there in black and white, the plot for her promotion and the role Bernard played in it. Leaping from the pages were the details of their first meeting at *WhisPer*. It was no coincidence. She read through every detail of the things Liz did to make her fall in love with her. How Liz played the victim to make Kayla sympathize with her. How she played on Kayla's broken heart to pull her in…it was all there…exactly as it had played out when they met.

Kayla's head felt as if she was being submerged under water as the details behind the reasons why Kayla was assigned

Alistair as a client emerged—the client whose money she would be accused of embezzling. Details of her daily movements, her calendar, her personal meetings and appointments; her social security number, information from her identification cards, driver's license, passport, it was all there…the information Liz used to set up an offshore account in her name.

But how did she get access to all this information? Kayla thought to herself as she shakenly continued to read through the pages. And then it all made sense—Lisa!—Her personal assistant. Liz had planted her into her life as well, Lisa had access to both her work and personal calendars. Lisa had access to her identification information. Lisa had information to almost everything.

The realization washed over like a cold dunking of water that she was being played by almost everyone she had trusted. Liz had them all in her pockets. *Oh my God, how naïve I was*, she all but whimpered at the evidence in her hands.

With shaking hands, she pulled her phone from her pocket and dialed James' number.

"It's all here," she said, as soon as James answered the phone. "Everything she has ever done, it's all here." Kayla's voice cracked with anxiety. "James your wife is a maniac!" Kayla's voice rose with terror. "I need to give this to the police and then I'm getting the hell away from you people," she ranted.

"Kayla!" James yelled, trying to get her to listen. "Where are you?"

"I'm at Liz, I found the journal in her study, it has everything and more. I can't believe I fell for someone so evil, so callous…."

"Kayla! If you have found the journal you need to get the hell out of there..." James yelled at her out of fear for what would happen if Liz returned to find her there in possession of the journal.

"I'm leaving now..." Kayla said. "With this journal I'll make sure she spends the rest of her miserable life in jail, paying for all the atrocities she has committed, all the lives she has ruined."

"Get out of the house now!"

Kayla turned to leave the study...and screamed. The phone fell out of her hand.

Liz was standing right there with a ghastly smirk on her face.

"Kayla! Kayla!" He shouted at the sound of her scream.

Liz stalked Kayla like a nocturnal predator after its prey. Her red hair wild and coiled at the ends, like little serpents, reminded Kayla of how Medusa must have looked.

"Oh Kayla," she said, her flinty green eyes fixed on the journal in Kayla's hand. "Did I underestimate you... love?" Her lips formed a semblance of a smile. "How long have you been on to me?" She said it in a dangerously elusive tone, that ignited Kayla's fear.

Kayla backed away from her holding on firmly to the journal.

"I see you have found my journal...with the help of James no doubt..." Liz continued with an ugly grimace that made Kayla's gut quiver.

"You two just can't seem to stay away from each other; which is the exact reason that one of you have to go."

"What have I ever done to you?" Kayla asked backing further away. "I told you how I met James, I had no idea that he was married, I would have never intentionally date a married man".

"Oh, save your pitiful whining for someone who cares!" Liz barked. "You are just as guilty as he is. You dated a man for so many years, who never seemed to have any intention of marrying you, who flies in and out of your life with shallow explanations and you never once questioned why? You never once questioned if he was seeing someone else? I figured out he was seeing someone else from the first year he left California for Vancouver. So why couldn't you? All in the name of being in love, being patient, being stupid! It is women like you that makes women seem weak, that make men feel like they can treat us anyway they please. Women like you make me sick! You were deceived because you allowed yourself to be deceived, and not just by James but by me."

Kayla backed away even farther as Liz got closer. She kept silent, paralyzed with fear.

"If you ask me I'm doing powerful woman like myself a favor and getting rid of the weaklings like yourself...the world has no room for women like you Kayla. I'm doing my part by eliminating you all, one bitch at a time."

Kayla was almost trapped now by the wall. Liz grinned wolfishly. "My mother was a strong woman...God rest her soul..." Liz continued in a false conversational manner. "See, I told you that my mother had died of natural causes in my last year of law school but that was far from the truth. Since you are either going to die here today or rot in jail for the rest of your miserable life,

I think I'll tell you the truth for once since we met. You see, I watched my mother build the empire that my father stole from underneath her. She made him into somebody, gave him power, wealth and affluence and he paid her back in lies and deceit, unable to keep his dick in his pants. By the time I got to high school, my father's adulterous ways took its toll on my mother, she became distant, withdrawn, broken and weak...because she loved him. I watched the powerful woman I couldn't one day wait to become wither away to nothing! She was in and out of one mental institution every other month from the series of break-downs and mental instability that my father's frolicking drove her to." Liz' eyes turned a murky green as she went back in time, rec-ollecting. "And when my father had succeeded in breaking her... stripping her of her true self...when she was at her weakest, he swooped in and he finished the job."

Kayla wanted to clamp her hands over her ears. She didn't want to hear the sordid details of what was bound to come next.

"I heard them arguing one evening when I got in from school, they didn't know I was there. I sneaked up and I watched as my father forced pills down my mom's throat and covered her nose and mouth suffocating her. She foamed from the mouth from the overdose of whatever pills my dad had forced her to take, and he held on to her, muffling her screams until her lifeless body collapsed on the floor."

The genesis of how this monster came into being was slowly unfolding to Kayla.

"I could have yelled, screamed even—but I didn't. Yes, my heart bled as I witnessed that my father had murdered her, but

I chose to be stronger than she was. I chose to avenge her in my own way. I was old enough to testify of what I had seen; but I couldn't allow him to get off that easy. He would probably go to jail but he wouldn't stay there, because he had what it took to be above the law. I stood over my mother's lifeless body when he left her there and I promised her that he would pay with his life...and he did...took me ten years to kill him but it was worth it, watching him suffer as my mom did," Liz cackled like a demented woman. Kayla suspected this was all to keep her in suspense as to her own fate.

"You see my father loved bourbon, more than he probably should, it was his weakness—he would go through a bottle of bourbon within hours. I did my research and I found a substance, untraceable, but deadly...a slow killer. I spent the next four years of my time in high school exacting my revenge, I laced his bottles of bourbon every day and night with just enough Botulinum to send his nervous system into the most excruciating pain known to man, but not enough to kill him quickly."

Kayla shook her head in disbelief as Liz droned on.

"I watched him suffer for years like my mom did, in and out of hospitals and no doctor could help him. Then I went to law school, and I continued to make him suffer while I prepped myself to rightfully take over my mother's legacy. When I got married and got pregnant with Charlotte, I decided it was time for him to go, I was satisfied and I knew my mother would have been proud of me for making him suffer a far worse fate than she did. I went to visit him one evening while I was heavily pregnant with Charlotte. He was pitiful, he wreaked of death, and he was no longer the high and mighty man that ruined my mother's life; that murdered my mother! I did him a favor that evening and took him out of his misery, I gave him the last glass of bourbon he would ever drink again in his miserable life with a deadly dose of Botulinum that finally caused his nervous system to fail and I watched as he died in extreme pain."

Kayla stared at her mutely, visibly shaking now.

"Lucky for me his heart also failed as his body was no longer strong enough to endure the pain, and so the doctors said he died from a heart attack. Poor daddy, she said in a mocking voice —"good riddance to bad rubbish..."

Kayla interjected, I don't need to hear any more of this. I need to go."

"Oh, you are going to hear it all my... love." She said the word with derision in her voice. "You see, my mom had made one dire mistake when she married my father...she married him because she loved him, not because he loved her...and I made damn sure not to make that mistake. I chose James because he loved me more than I had loved him, and I saw potential in him. I could mold him and make him into the man that I deserved, the man that I could eventually love. When I became pregnant with Charlotte I began to love him, but he was nowhere close to the man I needed him to be. I was in control of my marriage, what he did, where he went, how he dressed, who he spoke to, I was grooming him to be my perfect man, obedient, yet powerful and affluent."

"You're absolutely nuts," Kayla whispered.

"But James was weak and the moment he realized that he could not control me, he ran off to Vancouver where he met you. I knew all along what he was up to, and I let him have his fun, but all that ended the moment he fell in love with you. But I was lenient, I gave him a choice, you or Charlotte and he came back. He gave me his word that it was over. So, imagine my surprise when I realized that he was still in a relationship with you…he lied to my face, he took me for a fool; much like my father took my mom for a fool. So, I went a step further, I found out who my competition was…I did my research on you…only child, grew up most of your childhood without a mother, cared for by dear old daddy until you were old enough to make a life for yourself. Yet again, I gave James a choice, break it off or I would find you and destroy you. But you see—he may have left you physically back in Vancouver but he brought you back in his heart."

Kayla was overwhelmed by this jealous, hateful woman. Her lust for blood knew no bounds. "I don't know what you're talking about," Kayla shook her head back and forth.

"Well, if you don't, now you will know. Let me tell you," she wagged her finger at Kayla. "Every step of the way I spent the rest of my marriage competing with you for MY! husband's love. Do you know how it feels to hear your husband call another woman's name in his sleep?" She shouted.

"Do you know what I was going through knowing that my husband despised me but loved another? You have no idea… what that sort of thing can do to a woman's state of mind. But I wouldn't give him the gratification of seeing the pain he was putting me through. I remained strong, I had refused to let the weakness of a man weaken me." Liz leaned in closer to her, like a conspirator. "You see Kayla, James must pay for what he has done to me…but for him to truly experience the pain I felt when he chose you over his wife…then I need to stick him where it will hurt the most. It was clear to me…that he left you because he didn't want to see you get hurt, but he never got over you to this day. So, I figured it out…If I hurt you, he hurts…and the longer you suffer, the longer he suffers."

Tears streamed down Kayla's face and she pleaded, "but I'm innocent. I didn't know…"

"I'm going to break you down piece by piece, take everything away from you that made you into somebody who had the audacity to steal my husband's love away from me. I'm going to strip you of your career, your reputation, end even your freedom. You will spend the rest of your miserable life rotting in jail… and James—he will spend the rest of his miserable life blaming himself for it."

Liz moved closer to Kayla as she spouted her threats, Kayla said nothing else as fear took over her body. She knew she didn't deserve what Liz was going to do to her, but it was also obvious that Liz didn't care what she believed and wanted her to pay.

In a final attempt to stall Liz, Kayla asked in a shaky tone. "If you were planning to ruin my life all along or even kill me, why go through all this…I mean you got what you wanted you had me transferred to California, you had me exactly where you wanted me to frame me for fraud and embezzlement. So why cozy up to me, why make me fall in love with you, why did you get me a ring? Why did you propose to me? Why?" she cried in an agitated voice.

"I needed to study you." Liz responded in a still voice. "I needed to have you close to me where I could keep an eye on you, and what better way to do that unsuspiciously than to make you fall in love with me. I must admit though, the ring may have been a bit much, but I'm very theatrical if you haven't guessed it yet. Besides, when you were fucking my husband for all those years, weren't you yearning for him to propose to you? Were you not? So, I thought I would give you what you so desperately wanted from him all those years, I made an honest woman out of you." She giggled with an evil demented tone in her voice.

Kayla continued to move away going around the room in a circle, clutching on to the journal for dear life. Liz stopped at a lamp desk at a corner of her study and reached down for something,

Suddenly, she whipped out a gun and pointed it at Kayla.

"I'm going to need my journal back now," she said, her voice spent from all that talking. She jolted the gun at Kayla as she moved further away.

"I can't do that," Kayla said cowering. "I will not sit back and allow you to ruin my life without a fight. I do not deserve this!"

"Oh yes you do!" Liz screamed, banging the gun at the side of her head in a crazy fit. "You deserve everything that's coming. You may play the victim all you want, but let's face it Kayla, the fact of the matter is that you are the reason my husband left his family for all those years. You are the reason he stopped loving me! And you may lie to yourself that you are no longer in love with him, but I see right through you.

Wanna know a little secret Kayla? James is not the only one who calls out his lover's name in his sleep. You do too. The first time we made love at your house when I helped you move, that night you made love to James in your sleep right beside me. I watched you moan and caress yourself as you repeatedly called My! husband's name, and yet you stand here pretending that you no longer love him. How pathetic do you think I am?"

See, I knew that as soon as I divorced James he'd go running back to find you, so I decided, one of you had to go. And I chose you, because as much as James is a low-down dirty bastard; he's still the father of my children, and as callous as you may think I am, I will not let my children grow up without a father because of some bitch!"

But not to worry, James will get his...as I said, if you suffer, so will he. The choice is yours Kayla, a prison cell or a coffin, either way, I'll sleep just fine."

Kayla jolted her body further away from Liz, with a look on her face that showed Liz how crazy she thought she was. This made Liz even angrier, and she thrusted the gun at Kayla and screamed.

"You are not leaving this room with that journal Kayla. So, do yourself a favor and give it to me now. Or, I will shoot you and take it from your dead body!"

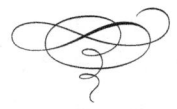

Chapter 16

"If you kill me you will go to jail. The police will know you did it!" Kayla said trying to call Liz's bluff.

"Oh Kayla," Liz said with a maniacal laugh, you really underestimate me, don't you?

"Don't forget, you broke into my house! That's all the police will care to know. I shot you in self-defense.

Do you want to know what my story to the police would be?" Liz asked in a calm yet deadly voice; and she started to recite her fake story to Kayla in the most believable and sincere manner.

"Oh officer, she had an affair with my husband and she wasn't happy when he broke it off. And when she had learnt that he had returned to California back to his family, she was determined to be with my husband that she requested to be transferred here to be closer to him.

But when she came here my husband still wouldn't have her...because he loved me. She became angry, enraged and more obsessed with my husband. She wanted him at all cost. And so, she planned to get rid of me. She stalked me for months, harassed me.

She somehow found out where I lived and she broke into my house. I came home from the market and she was in my house threatening to kill me for my husband. I feared for my life, and I ran to my study where I had my gun. She tried to stop me and we struggled and my gun went off. That's when I realized that she got shot...I had no choice...she tried to kill me..."

Liz ended her believable theatrics with a show of 'water works' and then gloatingly bowed for Kayla with a gratified laugh. She was good—and Kayla knew it She was screwed.

"Now give me the damn journal!" Liz screamed and pointed the gun at Kayla's chest. "You have two ways out of this and either of them won't end well for you, but either works for me... so what will it be...a body bag or spending the rest of your life in jail? Choose wisely," she taunted.

Kayla mustered up every bit of courage she had left. She had meant what she said; she would rather die trying to save her life. She looked Liz dead in the eye and yelled, "I choose neither!" With that said, she pranced on Liz as they both fell to the ground in a struggle.

Unknown to both of them, James had stayed on the line to realize that Liz had caught Kayla with the journal. He knew she was in danger, and so he had called the police while he rushed to Liz's house to prevent what he had feared would happen.

Liz and Kayla wrestled on the floor for what seemed like minutes. Kayla held on to Liz's hand with the gun, trying to prevent her from shooting. They both grunted and screamed from each other's blows.

Kayla got on top of Liz, trying to free her hand of the gun. In the middle of the struggle, the screams and the chaos there was a loud pop!

The gun went off.

Kayla had managed to get the gun from Liz but not before it went off….and suddenly there was complete silence.

James ran into the house at that very moment and he raced into Liz's study where he had heard the shot. The silence was suddenly broken by a chorus of sirens approaching in the distance.

When James burst into the study, Kayla was lying on top of Liz; the front of her white chiffon top stained in bright red blood. Her eyes bulged from the impact, her body then fell lifelessly to the floor, and the gun fell from her hands.

At the sight of Kayla's lifeless body on the floor, James let out a heart wrenching cry. "Noooooo! What have you done!" he yelled as he ran to Kayla's body—kicking the gun away from Elizabeth's reach.

"You are too late James," Liz smirked; panting from the struggle she had just had with Kayla. She quickly grabbed the journal and groggily tried to get up from the floor. The sound of sirens got louder as the police pulled up in the driveway.

James cradled Kayla's limp, unresponsive body in his arms as he cried…he then tried to apply pressure to her wound. "Help is on the way," he sobbed with bewilderment in his voice, "…just hold on…help is on the way."

At the sound of the police entering the house; Elizabeth tore the sleeves from her dress and banged her head against the desk to give herself a gash on the forehead—and started to shiver and cry.

James watched her in revulsion as he applied pressure to Kayla's wound. "In here!" He shouted, alerting the police to the room. "I need help, she's been shot!"

The Paramedics ran in and feverishly tried to get Kayla unto a stretcher and rushed her to the ambulance waiting outside. James followed desperately behind them and watched helplessly as they mounted her into the ambulance and sped off.

Inside the study Elizabeth began to act hysterical. "She broke into my house... she squealed...with tears running down her face. "...she tried to kill me... I had no choice....I shot her in self-defense."

James ran back to the house and he could hear Elizabeth bawling hysterically and spouting pure lies to the police. A police officer stopped James as he tried to re-enter the study. "Who are you sir?" the officer asked.

"I'm James...I called the police," he said, staring over at Elizabeth with hate in his eyes.

"I'm going to need a statement from you." The officer continued, taking James to a corner in the room.

"Everything she is claiming, it's all lies," he said looking over at Elizabeth.

"She's his mistress! Elizabeth shouted, playing the victim. He's trying to take her side!"

Unknowing to Elizabeth, James did not only stay on the line while she was detailing all her plans and threats against Kayla, he was also recording the entire time.

"It's all here," James said pulling out his phone. James started the recording and handed the phone to the officer. The recording had captured the entire conversation, everything the police needed to make an arrest.

Elizabeth was rendered speechless.

The officers read Elizabeth her rights as they handcuffed her. James also pointed them to the journal that Elizabeth had tried to stash behind the desk. James watched as they took her away in handcuffs and she looked at him as she walked by with a cold, detestable stare.

Fearing the worst, James rushed to his car and raced to the hospital. When he got there, he tried to see Kayla but doctors where still operating on her. He sat in the waiting room, fidgety and unsettled. Every now and then he got up from his seat, worriedly pacing up and down the corridors outside the operating room where they had Kayla.

Five hours later, a nurse came and got James and took him to the doctor who operated on Kayla. The doctor greeted James.

"We managed to get the bullet out without further damages to the point of entry. The bullet entered the left side of her chest, but luckily, it missed any major arteries and organs close by. "However," he continued, "she had lost a lot of blood at the shooting and a lot more during the operation. This forced us to place her in an induced coma for her body to fully recover without suffering any brain damage."

"A coma, you say?" James face turned ashen.

"From my medical experience, I can safely say that based on her age and her obvious impeccable state of health, she'll be out of the coma within the next couple of days."

The doctor then gave James access to Kayla's room and left him to be with her. James stayed by Kayla's bedside for the rest of the evening, assuring her that she would be ok, repeating what the doctor and told him, and apologizing over and over again.

At about 3 am the next day, James was awakened by a nurse who had come in to tend to Kayla. She told him to go home and get some rest and come back in the afternoon.

For the next two days. James spent most of the days by Kayla's side, willing her to wake up.

On day three as he sat beside her, holding onto her hand and stroking her face…he felt her finger move inside his grasp. She slowly opened her eyes and leaned to look at him.

Filled with excitement and relief, James yelled for the doctor. He waited anxiously as they examined Kayla and cleared her fit to leave the hospital within the next two days.

"You scared me," he said staring into her eyes. "I …I thought I had lost you…" He swallowed the ever-present lump in his throat.

Kayla said nothing—distraught, she looked into James' eyes. Tears flowed down her cheeks as the memory crashed in of what had transpired back in Liz's study.

With a faint voice, she asked James to get her phone so she could call her dad, and she asked him to leave the room so that she could have a private moment.

When James returned to the room he tried to continue to speak to Kayla, but her interest was not there...he took it as a que to leave and he did, assuring her that he was there for her and that he would be back in the morning.

The next day, James went back to the hospital, he hurriedly walked towards Kayla's room, smiling with excitement with a bouquet of flowers in his hands. But when he got there she was gone. He rushed outside and bumped into a nurse, he fervently tried to ask after Kayla.

"Yes...Miss Riviera..." the nurse replied, "she checked herself out this morning. I believe she left something for you." The nursed walked a confused James to the front desk where she brought out a white envelope.

He hesitantly took the envelope from her and walked to the waiting room where he sat down and opened it...inside was a note that read:

James,

If I have learned anything this past year, it's that I need to focus on myself. I have realized that all the times that I was vulnerable to the lies, and the deception of the people I had loved and trusted, was because I gave them all of me...I allowed myself to be hurt because I made myself believe that I needed someone to make me happy.

If I am ever to be truly happy, I need to distance myself from the things that caused me pain. And that means distancing myself from you, I no longer want to spend my life at the mercy of someone else's love. You left a hole in my heart that slowly started to heal when I met Elizabeth and before it could completely heal...she ripped it open again in the most horrendous of ways. It may be insensitive of me to say this...but in some ways you both deserve each other.

I have no more love to give James, I think it's time I let it all go. . .I need to find me again. I need to be happy—only for me, and so, this is me cutting the cord of whatever bizarre ties that had connected us before.

In all this craziness of your wife trying to kill me and all, you know what I realized? If she had never found out about us, you would have continued to lie to me for the rest of my life. You would have selfishly made yourself happy at the expense of my true happiness, because you knew from the beginning that you would never truly be mine. Don't you see James, you were never truly in love with me, you were in love with the traits I had that your wife had lost during your marriage.

What hurts the most is looking back I now understand that I was just a version of her to you, the version that you wanted back. My heart no longer beats for you James. . .finally I can stop lying to myself when I say that I feel nothing for you anymore.

If at this point in my letter you now suddenly find it hard to breathe from the knot in your throat, and if your heart suddenly feels as if it's going to burst out of your chest; if you suddenly feel like you have lost all reason to live. . .then I would have succeeded in making you experience what you did to me when you left.

And if you don't feel these emotions now, I hope that one day you will find yourself thinking back on all the memories we made.

I hope you ache in regret as the truth hits you like a bullet; that I once loved you more than anyone else in the entire world, and you nearly destroyed me.

Goodbye James.

. . .Forever.

THE END

Avagaye Clarke-Heron

Avagaye Clarke-Heron is a business professional by day and a writer by night as well as a wife and mom all year round. Jamaican born, she moved to the Cayman Islands in 2014 with her husband to pursue her career ambitions. Avagaye holds a Master's degree in General Management and a Bachelor's degree in Finance.

Avagaye has written a children's book and has also written a two-part romantic suspense series: *The Sweeter Side of Deception* which is book one to *Deception in the Details*.

Prior to starting her writing career, she experimented with various occupations: Property Management, Accounting, Retail Business Analyst... but her favorite job is the one she's now doing part time — writing romance.

Get the latest on author Avagaye Clarke-Heron
by emailing: InSpirePublications1@gmail.com
or subscribe on her website: www.inspirepublications.net

CHECK OUT BOOK ONE: *The Sweeter Side of Deception*
available at: amazon.com/author/inspirepub

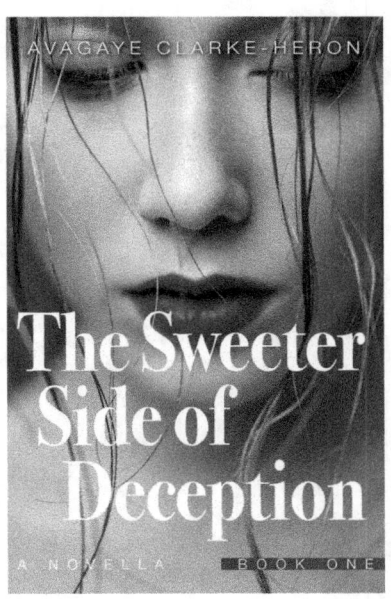

www.ingramcontent.com/pod-product-compliance
Lightning Source LLC
Chambersburg PA
CBHW060122260626
47160CB00005B/1975